TROUBLE ON
HER DOORSTEP

TROUBLE ON HER DOORSTEP

BY

NINA HARRINGTON

First published in Great Britain 2014
by Mills & Boon, an imprint of Harlequin (UK) Limited,
Large Print edition 2014
Eton House, 18-24 Paradise Road,
Richmond, Surrey, TW9 1SR

© 2014 Nina Harrington

ISBN: 978 0 263 24066 5

Printed and bound in Great Britain
by CPI Antony Rowe, Chippenham, Wiltshire

CHAPTER ONE

Tea, glorious tea. A celebration of teas from around the world.
There is no better way to lift your spirits than a steaming hot cup of builders' brew. Two sugars, lots of milk. White china beaker. Blend of Kenyan and Indian leaf tea. Brewed in a pot. Because one cup is never enough.

From *Flynn's Phantasmagoria of Tea*

Tuesday

'LADIES, LADIES, LADIES. No squabbling, please. Yes, I know that he was totally out of order but those are the rules. What happens in the Bake and Bitch club…?'

Dee Flynn lifted her right hand and waved it towards the women clustered about the cake display as though she was conducting a concert orchestra.

The women put down their tea cups, glanced at

one another, shrugged their shoulders and raised their right hands.

'Stays in the Bake and Bitch club,' a chorus of sing-song voices replied, a second before they burst into laughter and sank back into their chairs around the long pine table.

'Okay. I might not be able to snitch, but I still cannot believe that the faker tried to pass that sponge cake off as his own work,' Gloria sniggered as she poured another cup of Darjeeling and dunked in a homemade hazelnut biscotti. 'Every woman at the junior school bake sale knew that it was Lottie's triple-decker angel drool cake and you can hardly mistake that icing. We all know how hard it is to make, after last week's efforts.'

'Hey! Don't be so hard on yourself,' Lottie replied. 'That was one of my best recipes and chiffon sponge is not the easiest to get right. You never know; I might have become one dad's inspiration to greater things.'

A chorus of 'Boo,' and 'Not likely,' echoed around the table.

'Well, never mind about dads wanting to show off at the school bake sale in front of the other fabulous baked creations you gals create. We have five more minutes before your cakes come out of the oven so there is just enough time for you to taste my latest recipe for a February special. This is the cake I am going to demonstrate next week.'

With a flourish reserved for the finest award-winning restaurants where she and Dee had trained, Lottie Rosemount waited until every one of the girls had stopped talking and was looking at the cake plate at the centre of the table, before whipping away the central metal dome and revelling in the gasp of appreciation.

'Individual cupcakes. Dark chocolate and raspberry with white-chocolate hearts. And just in time for Valentine's Day. What do you think?'

'Think?' Dee coughed and took a long drink of tea. 'I am thinking that I have a week to come up with the perfect blend of tea to complement chocolate and raspberries.'

'Tea? Are you joking?' Gloria squealed. 'Hell no. Those cupcakes are not meant to be washed down with tea around the kitchen table. No chance. Those are after-dinner bedroom dessert cakes. No doubt about it. If I am lucky, I might get to eat half of one before my Valentine's Day dinner date gets really sweet—if you know what I mean. Girl, I want me some of those. Right now.'

A roar of laughter rippled like a wave around the room as Gloria snatched up a cupcake and bit into it with deep groans of pleasure, before licking her fingers. 'Lottie Rosemount, you are a temptation. If I made those cupcakes I know that I would get lucky, and just this once I would not think about the risk of chocolate icing on the bedclothes.'

Dee sniggered and had just pulled down a tea caddy of a particularly fragrant pomegranate infusion when she heard the distinctive sound of the antique doorbell at the front door of the tea rooms.

Lottie looked up from serving the cupcakes. 'Who can that be? We've been closed for hours.'

'Not to worry. I'll get it. But save one of those for me, can you? You never know—my luck might change and a handsome new boyfriend might turn up out of the blue just in time for Valentine's Day. Miracles can happen.'

Dee skipped out of the kitchen across the smooth wooden floorboards in her flat ballet pumps, and in three strides was inside the tea rooms. She flicked on the lights and instantly the long room was flooded with warm natural light which bounced back from the pistachio-and-mocha painted walls and pale wood fittings.

Lottie's Cake Shop and Tea Rooms had only been open a few months and Dee never got tired of simply walking up and down between the square tables and comfy chairs, scarcely able to believe that this was her space. Well, Lottie and Dee's space. They had each put up half of the money to get the business started. But they were partners sharing everything: tea and cake; both crazy, both working at the thing they loved best. Both willing to invest everything they had in this mad idea and take a risk that it would work.

Big risk.

A shiver ran across Dee's shoulders and she inhaled sharply. She needed this tea shop to work and work brilliantly if she had any hope of becoming a tea merchant in her own right. This was her last chance—her only chance—of creating some sort of financial future for herself and for her retired parents.

But suddenly the ringing bell was replaced by a hard rapping on the front door and she looked up towards the entrance. 'Hello? Is someone there?'

A male voice called out from the street in a posh English accent.

A tall dark figure was standing on the pavement on the other side of the door with his hands cupped over his forehead, peering at her through the frosted glass of the half-glazed door.

What a cheek! It was almost nine o'clock at night. He must be desperate. And it was lashing down with rain.

She took a step forward then paused and sniffed just once before striding on.

After a lifetime of travel she was not scared of a stranger knocking on her door. This was a London high street, for goodness' sake, not the middle of some jungle or tropical rain forest.

With a lift of her chin and a spring in her step, Dee turned the key in the lock in one smooth movement and pulled the front door sharply towards her.

A little too sharply, as it turned out.

Everything from that moment seemed to happen in slow motion—like in some freeze-framed DVD where you could scarcely believe what had happened, so you played the same scene over and over again in jerky steps, just to make sure that your memory was not playing tricks on you.

Because as she flung open the door, the very tall man just raised his arm to knock again and, in that split second he leant forward, he found the door was missing.

But his body carried on moving, carrying him forward into the tea room. And directly towards Dee, who had stepped backward to see who was knocking so loudly.

A pair of very startled blue-grey eyes widened as he tumbled towards her, the bright light almost blinding him after the gloomy dark street outside.

What happened next was Dee's fault. *All of it.*

Either time slowed down or her brain went into overdrive, because suddenly she had visions of lawyers claiming compensation for broken noses and bruised elbows. Or worse.

Which meant that she could not, dared not, simply leap out of the way and let this man, whoever he was, fall forward, flat on his face and hurt himself.

So she did the only thing she could think of in that split second.

She swept his legs out from under him.

It seemed to make perfect sense at the time.

Her left leg stepped forward to his left side as she reached up and grabbed hold of the soggy right sleeve of his rather elegant long dark-wool coat and pulled him towards her.

Then she swept her right leg out, hooked her ballet pump behind his left ankle and flipped him over sideways. By keeping a tight hold on his coat sleeve, even though it was wet and slimy, she took his weight so that instead of falling flat on his back his besuited bottom hit the wooden floor instead.

It was actually a rather good side judo foot sweep, which broke his fall and took his weight at the same time. Result!

Her old martial arts tutor would have been proud.

Shame that the two middle buttons on what she could now see was a very smart cashmere coat popped open with the strain and went spinning off onto the floor under one of the tables. But it was worth it. Instead of flying across the floor to join them, her male visitor sat down in a long, heavy slow slump instead. No apparent harm done.

Dee's fingers slowly slid away from the moist

fabric of his coat sleeve and his arm flopped down onto his knees.

She closed the front door and then sat back on her ankles on the floor so that she could look at him from about the same height.

And then look again.

Oh, my. Those blue-grey eyes were not the only thing that was startling. For a start he seemed to be wearing the kind of business suit she had last seen on the bank manager who had grudgingly agreed to give the bank loan on the tea room. Only softer and shinier and much, much more expensive. Not that she had much experience of men in suits, but she knew fabric.

And then there was the hair. The sleet had turned to a cold drizzle and his short dark-brown hair was curled into moist waves around his ears and onto his collar. Bringing into sharp focus a face which might have come from a Renaissance painting: all dark shadows and sharp cheekbones. Although the baggy tired eyes could probably use some of her special home-sewn tea bags to compensate for his late nights in the office.

Blimey! She had just swept the legs out from under the best looking man she had seen in a long time and that included the boys from the gym across the street, who stoked up on serious amounts of carbs before hitting the body-sculpting classes.

Men like this did not normally knock on her door....ever. Maybe her luck *had* finally changed for once.

A smile slid across Dee's mouth, before the sensible part of her brain which was not bedazzled by a handsome face decided to make an appearance.

So what was he doing here? And who was he?

Why not ask him and find out?

'Hello,' she said, peering into his face and telling her hormones to sit down. 'Sorry about that, but I was worried that you might hurt yourself when you fell into the shop. How are you doing down there?'

How was he doing?

Sean Beresford pushed himself up on one elbow and took a few seconds to gather his wits and refocus on what looked like a smart café or bistro, although it was hard to tell since he was sitting on the floor.

Looking straight ahead of him, Sean could

see cake stands, teapots and a blackboard which told him that the all-day special was cheese-and-leek quiche followed by an organic dark-chocolate brownie and as much Assam tea as he could drink.

Sean stared at the board and chuckled out loud. He could use some of that quiche and tea.

This was turning out to be quite a day.

It had started out in Melbourne what felt like a lifetime ago, followed by a very long flight, where he had probably managed three or four hours of sleep. And then there had been the joy of a manic hour at Heathrow airport where it soon became blindingly obvious that he had boarded the plane, but his luggage had not.

One more reason why he did not want to be sitting on this floor wearing the only suit of clothes that he possessed until the airline tracked down his bag.

Sean shuffled to a sitting position using the back of a very hard wooden chair for support, knees up, back straight, exhaled slowly and lifted his head.

And stared into two of the most startling pale-green eyes that he had ever seen.

So green that they dominated a small oval

face framed by short dark-brown hair which was pushed behind neat ears. At this distance he could see that her creamy skin was flawless apart from what looked like cake crumbs which were stuck to the side of a smiling mouth.

A mouth meant to appease and please. A mouth which was so used to smiling that she had laughter lines on either side, even though she couldn't be over twenty-five.

What the hell had just happened?

He shuffled his bottom a little and stretched out his legs. Nothing broken or hurting. That was a surprise.

'Anything I can get you?' The brunette asked in a light, fun voice. 'Blanket? Cocktail?'

Sean sighed out loud and shook his head at how totally ridiculous he must look at that moment.

So much for being a top hotel executive!

He was lucky that the hotel staff relying on him to sort out the disaster he had just walked into straight from the airport could not see him now.

They might think twice about putting their faith in Tom Beresford's son.

'Not at the moment, thank you,' he murmured with a short nod.

Her eyebrows squeezed tight together. She bent forward a little and pressed the palm of one hand onto his forehead, and her gaze seemed to scan his face.

Her fingers were warm and soft and the sensation of that simple contact of her skin against his forehead was so startling and unexpected that Sean's breath caught in his throat at the reaction of his body at that simple connection.

Her voice was even warmer, with a definite accent that told him that she has spent a lot of time in Asia.

'You don't seem to have a temperature. But it is cold outside. Don't worry. You'll soon warm up.'

It he did not have a temperature now, he soon would have, judging by the amount of cleavage this girl was flashing him as she leant closer.

Her chest was only inches away from his face and he sat back a little to more fully appreciate the view. She was wearing one of those strange slinky sweaters that his sister Annika liked to wear on her rare weekend visits. Only Annika wore a T-shirt underneath so that when it slithered off one shoulder she had something to cover her modesty.

This girl was not wearing a T-shirt and a tiny

strip of purple lace seemed to be all that was holding up her generously proportioned assets. At another time and definitely another place he might have been tempted to linger on that curving expanse of skin between the top of the slinky forest-green knit and the sharp collar bones and enjoy the moment, but she tilted her head slightly and his gaze locked onto far too many inches of a delicious-looking neckline.

It had been a while since he had been so very up close and personal to a girl with such a fantastic figure and it took a few seconds before what was left of the logical part of his brain clicked back into place. He dragged his focus a little higher.

'Nice top,' he grinned and pressed his hands against the floor to steady his body. 'Bit cold for the time of year.'

'Oh, do you like it?' She smiled and then looked down and gasped a little. In one quick movement she slid back and tugged at her top before squinting at him through narrow eyes. Clearly not too happy that he had been enjoying the view while she was checking his temperature.

'Cheeky,' she tutted. 'Is this how you normally

behave in public? I'm surprised that they let you out unsupervised.'

A short cough burst out of Sean's throat. After sixteen years in the hotel trade he had been called many things by many people but he had never once been accused of being cheeky.

The second son of the founder of the Beresford hotel chain did not go around doing anything that even remotely fell into the 'cheeky' category.

This was truly a first. In more ways than one.

'Did you just deck me?' he asked in a low, questioning voice and watched her stand up in one single, smooth motion and lean against the table opposite. She was wearing floral patterned leggings which clung to long, slender legs which seemed to go on for ever and only ended where the oversized sweater came down to her thighs. Combined with the green top, she looked like a walking abstract painting of a spring garden. He had never seen anything quite like it before.

'Me?' She pressed one hand to her chest and shook her head before looking down at him. 'Not at all. I stopped you from falling flat on your face and causing serious damage to that cute nose. You should be thanking me. It could have been a nasty fall, the way you burst in like that. This really is your lucky day.'

'Thank you?' he spluttered in outrage. Apparently he had a cute nose.

'You are welcome,' she chuckled in a sing-song voice. 'It is not often that I have a chance to show off my judo skills but it comes in handy now and then.'

'Judo. Right. I'll take your word for it,' Sean replied and looked from side to side around the room. 'What is this place?'

'Our tea rooms,' she replied, and peered at him. 'But you knew that, because you were hammering at our door.' She flicked a hand towards the entrance. 'The shop is closed, you know. No cake. No tea. So if you are expecting to be fed you are out of luck.'

'You can say that again,' Sean whispered, then held up one hand when she looked as though she might reply. 'But please don't. Tea and cakes are the last thing I came looking for, I can assure you.'

'So why were you hammering on the door, wearing a business suit at nine on a Tuesday evening? You have obviously come here for a reason.

Are you planning to sit on my floor and keep me in suspense for the rest of the evening?'

His green-eyed assailant was just about to say something else when the sound of female laughter drifted out from the back of the room.

'Ah,' she winced and nodded. 'Of course. You must be here to pick up one of the girls from the Bake and Bit…Banter club. But those ladies won't be ready for at least another half-hour.' One hand gestured towards the back of the room where he could hear the faint sound of female voices and music. 'The cakes are still in the oven.' Her lovely shoulders lifted in an apologetic shrug. 'We were late getting started. Too much bit…chatting and not enough baking. But I can tell someone you are here, if you like. Who exactly are you waiting for?'

Who was he waiting for? He wasn't waiting for anyone. He was here on a different kind of mission. Tonight he was very much a messenger boy.

Sean reached into the inside breast pocket of his suit jacket and checked the address on the piece of lilac writing paper he had found inside the envelope marked 'D S Flynn contact details' lying at the bottom of the conference room booking file. It had been handwritten in dark-green ink in very thin letters his father would instantly have dismissed as spider writing.

Well, he certainly had the right street and, according to the built-in GPS in his phone, he was within three metres of the address of his suspiciously elusive client who had booked a conference room at the hotel and apparently paid the deposit without leaving a telephone number or an email address. Which was not just inconvenient but infuriating.

'Sorry to disappoint you, but I am not here to pick up anyone from your baking club. Far from it. I need to track someone down in a hurry.'

He waved the envelope in the air and instantly saw something in the way she lifted her chin that suggested that she recognized the envelope, but she covered it up with a quizzical look.

That seemed to startle her and he could almost feel the intensity of her gaze as it moved slowly from his smart, black lace-up business brogues to the crispness of his shirt collar and silk tie. There was something else going on behind those green eyes, because she glanced back towards the entrance just once and then swung around towards the back of the room, before turning her attention on him again.

And when she spoke there was the faintest hint of concern in her voice which she was trying hard to conceal and failing miserably.

'Perhaps I could help if you told me who you were looking for,' she replied.

Sean looked up into her face and decided that it was time to get this over with so he could get back to the penthouse apartment at the hotel and collapse.

In one short, sharp movement he pushed himself sideways with one hand, curled his knees and effortlessly got back onto his feet, brushing down his coat and trousers with one hand. So that, when he replied, his words were more directed towards the floor than the girl standing watching him so intently.

'I certainly hope so. Does a Mr D S Flynn live here? Because, if he does, I really need to speak to him. And the sooner the better.'

CHAPTER TWO

Tea, glorious tea. A celebration of teas from around the world.
'A woman is like a tea bag: you never know how strong it is until it's in hot water.' Eleanor Roosevelt.

From *Flynn's Phantasmagoria of Tea*

'WHAT WAS THAT name again?' Dee asked, holding on to the edge of the counter for support, in a voice that was trembling way too much for her liking. 'Mr Deesasflin. Was that what you said? Sounds more like a rash cream. It is rather unusual.'

A low sigh of intense exasperation came from deep inside his chest and he stopped patting down his clothes and stretched out tall. As in, very tall. As in well over six feet tall in his smart shoes which, for a girl who was as vertically challenged as she was, as Lottie called it, seemed really tall.

Worse.

He was holding the envelope that she had given to the hotel manager the first time she had visited the lovely, posh, boutique hotel to suss out the conference facilities.

They had gone through everything in such detail and double-checked the numbers when she had paid the deposit on the conference room in October.

So why was this man, this stranger, holding that envelope?

Dee racked her brains. Things had been pretty mad ever since Christmas but she would have remembered a letter or call from the hotel telling her that it had been taken over or they had appointed a new manager.

Who made house calls.

Oh no, she groaned inside. This was the last thing she needed. Not now. *Please tell me that everything to do with the tea festival is still going to plan...please?* She had staked her reputation and her career in the tea trade on organizing this festival. And the last of her savings. Things had to be okay with the venue or she would be toast.

'Flynn. D. S.' His voice echoed out across the

empty tea room, each letter crisp, perfectly enunciated and positively oozing with annoyance. 'This letter was all that I could find in the booking system. No name or telephone number or email address. Just an address, a surname and two initials.'

What? All that he could find?

Great. Well, that answered that question: he was from the hotel.

She was looking at her gorgeous but grumpy new hotel manager or conference organizer.

Who she had just sideswiped.

Splendid. This was getting better and better.

The only good news was that he seemed to think that his client was a man, so she could find out the reason for his obvious grumpiness without getting her legs swiped from under her. With a bit of luck.

As far as he knew, she was just a girl in a cake shop. Maybe she could keep up the pretence a little longer and find out more before revealing her true credentials.

'You don't seem very pleased with this Mr Flynn person.' She smiled, suddenly desperate to appear as though she was just an outside party making conversation. 'They must have done something seriously outrageous to make you come out on a wet night in February to track them down.'

Ouch. That was such a horrible expression. The idea that he had made it as far as the tea rooms and was actually hunting her was enough to give her an icy cold feeling in the pit of her stomach which was going to take a serious amount of hot tea to thaw out.

From the determined expression on his face, right down to the very official business suit and smart haircut, this man spelt 'serious'.

As serious as all of the finance people who had tried their hardest to crush her confidence and convince her that her dream was a foolish illusion. She had been turned down over and over again, despite the brilliant business plan she had worked on for weeks, and all the connections in the tea trade that she could ever need.

The message was always the same: they could not see the feasibility of a new tea import business in the current economy. All of the statistics about the British obsession with tea and everything connected with it had seemed to fly over their heads. Not enough profit. Too risky. Not viable.

Was it any wonder that she had gone out on a

limb and offered to organize the tea festival so that she could launch her import business at the same time?

Lottie had been her saviour in the end and had pulled in a few favours so that the private bank her parents used was aware that it was a joint business with the lovely, seriously wealthy and connected Miss Rosemount as well as the equally lovely but seriously broke Miss Flynn.

Come to think of it, the banker had been a girl in a suit. But a suit all the same.

'On the contrary, Mr Flynn has not done anything. But I do need to speak to him as soon as possible.'

'May I take a message?' she asked in her best 'innocent bystander' voice, and smiled.

He paused for a second and she thought that he was going to slide over to her counter but he was simply straightening his back. Oh lord. Another two inches taller.

'I am sorry but this is a confidential business matter for my client. If you know where I can find him, it is important that we talk on a very urgent matter about his booking.'

A cold, icy pit started to form in the base of

Dee's stomach and something close to panic flitted up like a bucket of cold water splashed over her face.

She blinked, lifted her chin and stuck out her hand. 'That's me. Dervla Skylark Flynn. Otherwise known as Dee. Dee S Flynn. Tea supplier to the stars. I'm the person you are looking for, Mr...?'

He took two long steps to cross the room and shake her hand. A real handshake. His long, slender fingers wrapped around her hand which Dee suddenly realized must be quite sticky from dispensing cake and biscuits and clearing away bowls covered in cake batter.

His gaze was locked on her face as he spoke, and she could almost see the clever cogs interconnecting behind those blue eyes as he processed her little announcement, took her word that she was who she said she was and went for it without pause.

Clever. *She liked clever.*

'Sean Beresford. I am the acting manager of the Beresford Hotel, Richmond Square. Pleased to meet you, Miss Flynn.'

'Richmond Square?' She replied, trying to keep

the panic out of her voice. 'That's the hotel where I booked a conference room for February. And...'

Then her brain caught up with the name he had given her and she inhaled through her nose as his fingers slid away from hers and rested lightly on the counter.

'Did you just say Beresford? As in the Beresford family of hotel owners?'

A smile flickered across his lips which instantly drew her gaze, and her stupid little heart just skipped a beat at the transformation in this man's face that one simple smile made.

Lord, he was gorgeous. Riveting.

Oh, smile at me again and make my blood soar. Please?

And now she was ogling. How pathetic. Just because she was within touching distance of a real, live Beresford did not mean that she had to go to pieces in front of him.

So what if this man came from one of the most famous hotel-owning families in the world? A Beresford hotel was a name splashed across the broadsheet newspapers and celebrity magazines, not *Cake Shop and Tea Room Weekly*.

This made it even more gut-clenching that he

had just been in close and personal contact with her floorboards.

'Guilty as charged,' he replied and touched his forehead with two closed fingers in salute. 'I am in London for a few months and the Richmond Square hotel is one of my special projects.'

'You're feeling guilty?' she retorted with a cough. 'What about me? You almost had an accident here tonight. And I could have dropped you. Oh, that is so not good. Especially when you have come all the way from the centre of London late in the evening to see me.'

Then she shook her head, sucked in a long breath and carried on before he had a chance to say anything. 'Speaking of which, now we have the introductions sorted out, I think you had best tell me what the problem is. Because I am starting to get scared about this special project you need to see me about so very urgently.'

He gestured towards the nearest table and chairs.

'You may need to sit down, Miss Flynn.'

A lump the size of Scotland formed in her throat, making speech impossible, so she replied with a brief shake of the head and a half-smile and gestured to one of the bar stools next to the tea bar.

She watched in silence as he unbuttoned his coat, scowled at the missing buttons then sat down on the stool and turned to face her, one elbow resting on the bar.

Nightmare visions flitted through her brain of having to tell the tea trade officials that the London Festival of Tea was going to going to be cancelled because she had messed up booking the venue, but she fought them back.

Not going to happen. That tea festival was going ahead even if she had to rent the damp and dusty local community centre and cancel the bingo night.

She had begged the tea trade organization to give her the responsibility for organizing the event and it had taken weeks to convince the hardened professionals that she could coordinate a major London event.

Everything she had worked for rested on this event being a total success. *Everything.*

Suddenly the room started to feel very warm and she dragged over a bar stool and perched on it to stop her wobbly legs from giving way under her.

Focus, Dee. Focus. It might not be as bad as she was thinking.

'I only took over the running of the hotel today so it has taken me a while to go through all of the paperwork. That's why I only started working through the conference-booking system this afternoon. I apologize for not calling in earlier but there has been a lot of catching up to do and I didn't have any contact details.'

She swallowed down her anxiety. 'But what happened to the other manager? Frank Evans? He was taking care of all my arrangements in person and seemed very organized. I must have filled in at least three separate forms before I paid the deposit. Surely he has my contact details?'

'Frank decided to take up a job offer with another hotel company last Friday. Without notice. That's why I came in to sort out the emergency situation at Richmond Square and get things back on track.'

She gasped and grabbed his arm. 'What kind of emergency do you have?' Then she gulped. 'Has something happened? I mean, has the hotel flooded or—' she suddenly felt faint '—burnt down? Gas explosion? Water damage?'

'Flooded?' he replied, then tilted his head a tiny fraction of an inch. 'No. The hotel is absolutely fine. In fact, I went there straight from the airport and it is as lovely as ever. Business as usual.'

'Then please stop scaring the living daylights out of me like that. I don't understand. Why is there a problem with the booking?'

'So you met Frank Evans? The previous manager?'

She nodded. 'Twice in person, then I spoke to him several times over the phone. Frank insisted on taking personal responsibility for my tea festival and we went over the room plans in detail. Then we had lunch at the hotel just before Christmas to make sure that everything was going to plan. And it was. Going to plan.'

'In any of those meetings, did you see him recording any of your details on a diary or paper planner? Anything like that?

'Paper? No. Now that you mention it, I don't remember him taking any notes on paper. It was all on his notebook computer. He showed the photos of the layout on the screen. Is that a problem? I mean, isn't everything loaded onto computers these days?'

There was just enough of a pause from the

man looking at her to send a shiver across Dee's shoulders.

'Okay; I get the picture. How bad is it?' she whispered. 'Just tell me now and put me out of my misery.'

'Frank may have taken your details but he didn't load them onto the hotel booking system. If he had, Frank would have found out that we were already double-booked for the whole weekend with a company client who had booked a year in advance. So you see, he should never have accepted your booking in the first place. I am sorry, Miss Flynn, I have to cancel your booking and refund your deposit... Miss Flynn?'

But Dee was already on her feet.

'Stay right where you are. I need serious cake washed down with strong, sugary tea. And I need it now. Because there is no way on this planet that I am going to cancel that booking. No way at all. Are we clear? Good. Now, what can I get you?'

'I don't understand it. Frank seemed so confident and in control,' Dee said in a low voice. 'And he loved my oolong special leaf tea and was all excited about the conference. What happened?'

Sean was siting opposite and she watched him sip the fragrant Earl Grey that Dee had made for him. Then took another sip.

'This is really very good,' Sean whispered, and wrapped his fingers around the china beaker.

'Thank you. I have a wonderful supplier in Shanghai. Fifth-generation blender. And you still haven't answered my question. Is it a computer problem? It was, wasn't it? Some crazy, fancy booking system that only works if you have a degree in higher mathematics?'

She waved the remains of a very large piece of Victoria sandwich cake through the air. 'My parents were right all along: I should never trust a man who did not carry paper and pen.'

She paused with her cake half between her mouth and her plate and licked her lips.

'Do you have paper and a pen, Mr Beresford?'

He reached into the inside pocket of his suit jacket and pulled out a state-of-the-art smart phone.

'Everything I type is automatically synched with the hotel systems and my personal diary. That way, nothing gets lost or overlooked. Which makes it better than a paper notepad which could be misplaced.'

Dee peered at the glossy black device covered with tiny coloured squares and then shook her head. 'Frank didn't have one of those. I would have remembered.'

'Actually, he did. But he chose not to use it.' Sean sighed. 'I found it still in the original packaging in his office desk this afternoon.'

'Ah ha. Black mark for Team Beresford Hotels. Time for some staff training, methinks.'

'That's why I am back in London, Miss Flynn.' Sean bristled and put away his phone and started refastening his remaining coat buttons. 'To make sure that this sort of mistake does not happen again. I will personally arrange to have your deposit refunded tomorrow so you can organize a replacement venue at your convenience.'

She looked at him for a second then took another swig of very dark tea before lowering her large china beaker to the table. Then she stood up, stretched and folded her arms.

'Which part of "I am not cancelling" did you not understand? I don't want my deposit back. I want my conference suite. No, that's not quite right.'

Her eyebrows squeezed tight together. 'I *need* my conference room. And you…' she smiled up at him and fluttered her eyelashes outrageously '… are going to make sure I get it.'

Sean sighed, long and low. 'I thought that I had made it clear. The conference facilities at the Richmond Square had already been reserved for over a year before Frank accepted your booking. There are four hundred and fifty business leaders arriving from all over the world for one of the most prestigious environmental strategy think-tank meetings outside Davos. Four days of high-intensity, high-profile work.'

'Double-booked. Yes. I understand. But here is the thing, Sean; you don't mind if I call you Sean, do you? Excellent. The lovely Frank made my copies of all of those forms I signed on his very handy hotel photocopier and, as far as I know, my contract is with the Beresford hotel group. And that means that you have to find me an alternative venue.'

'But that is quite impossible at this short notice.'

And then he did it.

He looked at her with the same kind of condescending and exasperated expression on his face as her high school headmistress had used when she'd turned up for her first big school experience in London after spending the first fifteen years of her life travelling around tea-growing estates in India with her parents.

'Poor child,' she had heard the teacher whisper to her assistant. 'She doesn't understand the complicated words that we are using. Shame that she has no chance in the modern educational system. It's far too late for her to catch up now and get the qualifications she needs. *What a pity she has no future.*'

A cold shiver ran down Dee's back just at the memory of those words. If only that teacher knew that she had lit a fire inside her belly to prove just how wrong she had been to write her off as a hopeless case just because she had been outside the formal school system. And that fire was still burning bright. In fact, at this particular moment it was hot enough to warm half the city and certainly hot enough to burn this man's fingers if he even tried to get in her way.

This man who had fallen into her tea rooms uninvited was treating her like a child who had to be tolerated, patted on the head and told to keep quiet while the grown-ups decided what was going to happen to her without bothering to ask her opinion.

This handsome man in a suit didn't realize that he was doing it.

And the hair on the back of her neck flicked up in righteous annoyance.

She had never asked to come to London. Far from it. And what had been her reward for being uprooted from the only country that she had called home?

Oh yes. Being ridiculed on a daily basis by the other pupils because of her strange clothes and her Anglo-Indian accent, and then humiliated by the teachers because she had no clue about exam curricula and timetables and how to use the school desktop computers. Why should she have? That had never been her life.

And of course she hadn't been able to complain to her lovely parents. They were just as miserable and had believed that they were doing the right thing, coming back to Britain for the big promotion and sending her to the local high school.

Well, that was then and this was now.

The fifteen-year-old Dee had been helpless to

do anything about it but work hard and try to get through each day as best as she could.

But she certainly did not have to take it now. She had come a long way from that quiet, awkward teenager and worked so very hard to put up with anything less than respect.

Maybe that was why she stepped forward and glared up into his face so that he had to look down at her before he could reply.

'Exactly. There is no way that I could find another hotel that can cope with three hundred international tea specialists less than two weeks before the festival. Everywhere will be booked well ahead, even in February.'

She lifted her cute little chin and stared him out. 'Here is a question for you: would you mind reminding me exactly how many hotels the Beresford hotel group runs in London? Because they seem to be popping up everywhere I look.'

'Five,' he replied in a low voice.

'Five? Really? That many? Congratulations. Well, in that case it shouldn't be any trouble for you to find me a replacement conference room in one of the four other hotels in our fine city. Should it?' she said in a low, hoarse voice, her eyes locked onto his. And this time she had no intention of looking away first.

The air between them was so thick with electricity that she could have cut it with a cake knife. Time seemed to stretch and she could see the muscles in the side of his face twitching with suppressed energy, as though he could hardly believe that she was challenging him.

Because she had no intention whatsoever of giving in.

No way was she going to allow Sean Used-to-having-his-own-way Beresford to treat her like a second-class citizen.

And the sooner he realized that, the better!

Sean felt the cold ferocity of those pale-green eyes burn like frostbite onto his cheeks, and was just about to tell her what an impossible task that was when there was an explosion of noise and movement from behind his back. What seemed like a coach party of women of all shapes and ages burst out into the tea rooms, laughing like trains, gossiping and competing with one another in volume and pitch to make their voices heard above the uproar.

It felt like a tsunami of women was bearing down on him.

All carrying huge bags bursting with what looked like cake tins and mystery utensils and binders. Sean stepped back and practically squeezed himself against one wall to let the wall of female baking power sweep past him towards the entrance and out into the street.

'Ah, Lottie. There you are!' Dee Flynn cried out and grabbed the sleeve of a very pretty slim blonde dressed in a matching navy T-shirt and trousers. 'Sorry I did not get back to serve more tea. Come and meet Sean. The London Festival of Tea is going to have a new exciting venue and Sean here is the man who is in charge of finding the perfect location. And he is not going to rest until he has found the perfect replacement.'

She grinned at him with an expression of pure delight, with an added twist of evil. 'Aren't you, Sean?'

CHAPTER THREE

Tea, glorious tea. A celebration of teas from around the world.

There are many different kinds of tea, but they are all derived from just one type of plant: *Camellia sinensis*. The colour and variety of the tea (green, black, white and oolong) depends on the way the leaves are treated once they are picked.

From *Flynn's Phantasmagoria of Tea*

Wednesday

'SO HOW ARE you enjoying being back in London?' Rob Beresford's voice echoed out from the computer screen in his usual nonchalant manner. His eyebrows lifted. 'Same old madness?'

'Nothing that boring.' Sean snorted and pointed to the bags under his eyes. 'Still shattered. Still jet-lagged. Still wading through the mess Frank Evans got himself into at Richmond Square. I still can't believe that the man we trusted to run our hotel just took off and left this disaster for someone else to sort out.'

Sean's half-brother sat back in his chair and gave a low cough. 'Now, who does that remind me of? Oh yes, your ex-girlfriend. I caught up with the lovely Sasha at the catering-strategy forum last week. She asked me to say hi, by the way. Now, wasn't that sweet? Considering that she dumped you with zero notice. I could almost dislike her if it wasn't for her fantastic figure.' Rob gave a low, rough sigh. 'And that tan… She's looking good, brother. The Barbados hotel seems to be suiting her very nicely and the clients love her.'

'Thanks for the update.' Sean coughed and then squinted towards the computer screen. 'And she did not dump me. It simply wasn't working out for either of us. Trying to co-ordinate our diaries so that we were in the same time zone for more than a few days had stopped being funny a long time before we called it a day. You know what chaos it was last year! You were there, working the same hours as I was.'

Sean turned back to shuffling through a file on the desk. Sasha had been on the fast-track Beresford Hotels management programme and he had been working so hard that he hadn't even noticed that they barely saw one another face to face any more.

Until he'd come back to her apartment at one a.m., exhausted after two weeks on the road solving all the teething problems for a hotel opening, to find Sasha sitting waiting for him.

He had just missed her birthday dinner, the one he had promised that he would be there for. Not even the private jet could fly in tropical storms.

It was a pity that it hadn't been the first time that he'd missed her birthday. They had both worked like crazy over the Christmas and New Year holiday, but February should have been down time. Until the new hotel they were opening in Mexico had flooded only days before the grand opening and a holiday became a distant memory.

They had talked through the night but in the end there had been no escaping the truth. He was the operations troubleshooter and Tom Beresford's son. It was his job to be on stand-by and cope with emergencies. No matter what else was happening in his life. Or who. And she'd wanted more than he was prepared to give her.

It had been crunch time. He could either decide to give her the commitment she needed and deserved or they could walk away as friends who had enjoyed a fun and light hearted relationship and leave it like that.

He had not even bothered to unpack.

'Ah, but I still managed to find the time to enjoy the company of a few lovely ladies,' Robert replied. 'Unlike some people. But that's past history. So last year! Come on; you were in Australia for six weeks scouting for new locations! You must have spent some time at the beach.'

Robert Beresford sat back with his hands clasped behind his head. 'I am having visions of lovely ladies in very small bikinis on golden sands and surf boards. Classy. You have just made my day.'

'I know. I can see you drooling from here,' Sean shook his head. 'That was the plan. Two glorious weeks in Melbourne in February. Two weeks to sleep, soak up the sun and generally have some down time before starting the Paris assignment.'

He waved the conference-booking file at the screen. 'That *was* the plan. And now I am in London instead. Remind me again why I am the one who gets called in to pick up the pieces when the brown stuff hits the fan?'

'Who else is the old man going to call? I am only interested in the food and drink side of this crazy business, remember? There has to be someone in the family who can squeeze into a super-hero costume and fly in to save the day and Annika is way too stylish to wear underpants over her tights.'

Sean laughed out loud and flicked open the event files. 'Now, that is just being mean. I caught those last restaurant reviews. The food critics are crazy about that new fusion franchise you brought in. Kudos.'

Rob saluted him with a hat-tip. 'I'll tell you all about it when we meet up for the conference on Friday. Right? And try and relax. You'll have that mess sorted out by then. You always do. Shame that you can't take some down time before starting the new job. But you never know. You might find some sweet distraction while you are in London.'

Then Sean's gaze caught the lilac envelope that he had popped onto his desk to be filed. He quickly stole a glance at the file he had updated the minute he had got back to his hotel room the previous evening. Complete with the photo of Dee he had clipped from a London newspaper article from the previous October about the opening of Lottie's Cake Shop and Tea Rooms.

The two girls were standing outside the cake shop in what looked to be a cold autumn day.

Dee grinned out to the photographer with a beaming smile which was a lot warmer than the one he had been on the receiving end of. But her colour scheme was just as alarming.

She was wearing a short, pleated green skirt in a loud check-pattern tweed and a knitted top in fire-engine red partly covered with a pretty floral apron. Her blonde friend, Lottie, was in navy trousers and top with the same apron and compared to Dee looked elegant, sedate and in control while Dee looked…like a breath of fresh air. Animated, excited and alive.

That was the strange thing. Even in a digital scan from a newspaper this girl's energy and passion seemed to reach out from the flat screen, grab him and hold him tight in her grasp. She was looking at him right in the eyes. Just as she had in the flesh. No flinching or nervous sideways glances. Just single-minded focus, with eyes the colour of spring-green leaves; it was quite impossible to look away.

But not cold. Just the opposite, in fact. Even when she'd been challenging him to come up with a replacement venue that sexy smile was warm enough to turn up the heat on a cold winter's evening. Or was it that slippery one-shoulder sweater that she had been almost wearing?

He had vowed never to get involved in another relationship after Sasha, and no amount of bar crawling with Rob had persuaded him to change his mind. But there was something about Dee that seemed to get under his skin and he couldn't shake it off.

Maybe it was getting very up close to a client when he had no clue who she was?

It was usual practice in Beresford hotels for the conference manager to take a photo of their client so that the team could recognize who they were dealing with.

Sean blinked and cricked back his neck, which was stiff from stress and lack of sleep. Jet lag. That was it. He had a workload which was not funny and two weeks in London before heading to his new job in Paris. He didn't have time to sort out double bookings and track down conference space in the London hotels.

If only Frank had followed procedures!

'You wouldn't be calling me Superman if you had seen me last night,' he chuckled, then blinked and looked up at the monitor, where Rob was tapping his pen and looking at him with a curious expression.

'Do tell.'

'A girl with green eyes and a wicked judo throw brought me to my knees. That's all I am going to say.'

Rob snorted and sat forward with his elbows on the desk, and that gleam in his eyes which had got both of them into trouble on more than one occasion. 'Now that really is being mean. I need facts, a photograph and vital statistics. Sounds like the kind of girl I would like to meet. In fact, here is an idea—free, gratis and no charge. Bring this green-eyed fiend to the management dinner on Friday night. If you think you can handle it? Or should I have security on standby?'

'What…so you can ogle the poor girl all evening? No way.'

'Then give me something to report back to Annika in the way of gossip. You know she is always trying to set me up with her pals. It's about time our sister focused on you for a change. Are you planning on seeing this girl again?'

Sean checked the clock on the computer screen.

'As a matter of fact, I am meeting up with her this morning. Our latest client has given me a mission and I have a feeling that this lady is not going to fobbed off with anything but the best. In fact, come to think of it, I might need that super-hero costume after all.'

'How about this one?' Dee called out as Lottie swept by with a tray of vanilla-cream pastry slices. '"Flynn's Phantasmagorian Emporium of Tea".'

Then she leant back and peered at the words she had just written in chalk on the 'daily specials' blackboard next to the tea and coffee station.

'It has a certain ring to it and I can just see it on a poster. Maybe dressed up in a Steampunk theme. I like it!'

Lottie gave two short coughs, continued filling up the tiered cake stand on the counter then waved to two of their favourite breakfast customers as they strolled out onto the street.

'You also liked "Flynn's Special Tea Time Fantasies", until I pointed out that some folks might get the wrong idea and think you are selling a different kind of afternoon fantasy experience where you are not wearing much in the way of clothing. And I don't know about you, but I am not quite that desperate to sell your leaf teas.'

'Only people with that kind of mind.' Dee tutted. 'Shame on a nice well-brought-up girl like you for thinking such things.'

'Just trying to keep you out of mischief. Again.'

Dee felt the weight of an unexpected extra layer of guilt settle on her shoulders and she slipped off her stool and gave Lottie a one-armed hug. She had been so focused on organizing the festival that Lottie had done a lot more work than she should have done in the shop. 'Thanks for putting up with me. I know I can be a tad obsessive now and then. I don't know what I would have done without you these past months. Organizing this tea festival has already taken so much of my time; I'm sure that you have done more than your fair share in the shop.'

'That's okay.' Lottie grinned and hugged her back. 'It takes one obsessive to know one, right? Why else do you think I came to you the minute I had the idea for a cake shop? I needed someone who loved tea.'

Lottie stood back and nodded towards the blackboard with the daily specials. 'Tea. Cake. Gotta be a winner.' Then she turned back to the cake stand. 'Turns out that I was right.'

'Any chance that you could sprinkle some of that business-fairy dust in this direction? I am going to need something to give my own special blend of afternoon tea that special oomph, or I'll never make any money out of the tea festival.'

Dee slumped down on her stool and stared out at the breakfast customers who were slurping down her English breakfast tea with Lottie's almond croissants and ham and cheese paninis.

Lottie strolled over and sat down next to her before replying. 'I know that I promised not to get involved, because we agreed that it is important that you do this on your own, but what about all of the exhibitors who will be selling their teas and chinaware and teapots and special tea kettles and the like? Surely they're giving you a fee or a cut in any sales they make on the day?'

'They are. But it's just enough to cover the money I spent on the deposit for the hotel. Beresford is really expensive, even for one day. But I thought that a big international hotel chain like Beresford wouldn't let me down, so it was worth paying for the extra security just to make that there wouldn't be any last minute hassles with the venue. Hah! Wrong again.'

Dee started tapping her tea spoon on the counter. 'After Mr B left I called Gloria to ask if the church hall might be available. The ladies' lunch club loved my last demonstration on tea tasting. I thought that Gloria could put a good word in for me and I might even get it for free. But do you know what? Even the church hall is fully booked for the rest of the month.'

'I thought you said that it was damp and there were mouse droppings in the kitchen,' Lottie replied as she cut two large slices from a coffee-walnut layer cake and tastefully arranged them on the cake stand.

'Yes and yes. Small details. But that settles it;

Sean Beresford is going to have to find me a mega replacement venue. Whether he likes it or not.'

'Well, you did have one bonus. The lovely Sean. In the flesh. I didn't think that the millionaire heirs to the Beresford hotel chain turned up in person to break bad news, so he scores a few points on the Rosemount approval board. And, oh my—tall, dark and handsome does not come close. And he seemed very interested in you. I think that you might be on to a winner there.'

The memory of a pair of sparkling blue eyes smiling down at her tugged at the warm and cuddly part of Dee's mind and her traitorous heart gave just enough of a flutter to make her cover up her smirk with a quick sniff.

Dee pressed her lips together and shook her head. 'Charlotte Rosemount, you are such a total romantic. Can I remind you where that has taken us in the past? I lost track of the number of frogs we had to kiss back at catering college before you finally admitted that not one of those boys was a prince. And then you had the cheek to set me up with Josh last year.'

'It was a simple process of elimination!' Lottie grinned and then twisted her face into a grimace.

'I did get it wrong about Josh, though. He looked so good on paper! His dad was even a director at the tea company and he had the looks to die for. But sheesh, what a loser he turned out to be.'

'Exactly!' Dee nodded. 'And it took me six months to find out that all he wanted was a stand-in girl until someone more suitable came along. No, Lottie. Handsome hotel owners do not date girls who deck them. Well-known fact. Especially girls who give them extra work and refuse to go along with their get-rid-of-the-annoyance-as-quickly-as-possible schemes.'

'Perhaps he likes a girl who can stand up him. You are a change from all of the gold-diggers who hit on him on a daily basis. And he liked your Earl Grey.'

'Please. Did you see him? That suit cost more than my last shipment of Oolong. That is a man who fuels up on espressos and wouldn't let carbs pass his lips. He will pass the problem on to someone else to sort out, you wait and see. Big fish, small pond. Passing through on the way to greater things. Just like Josh. I think he only turned up to tell me so that he could tick me off his to-do list.'

'But he is trying to find you a replacement venue. Isn't he?'

'His assistant is probably run off her feet at this minute calling every hotel in London which is still available on a Saturday two weeks before the event. The list will be small and the hotels grotty. And he is not getting away with it. I need a high-class venue and nothing else will do.'

Lottie was just about to reply when the telephone rang on the wall behind them and the theme song for *The Teddy Bears' Picnic* chimed out. She scowled at Dee, who shrugged as though she had not been responsible for changing the ring tone. Again.

'Lottie's Cake Shop and Tea Rooms,' Lottie answered in her best professional voice, and then she reached out and grabbed Dee by the sleeve, tugging hard to make sure that she had her full attention. 'Good morning to you, too, Sean. Why yes, you are in luck, she is right here. I'll just get Dee for you.'

Lottie opened her mouth wide, baring her very white teeth, and held out the telephone towards Dee, who took it from her as Lottie picked up a menu and fanned her face. The message was only too clear: hot.

Dee looked at the caller ID on the phone for second longer than necessary and lifted her chin before speaking.

Time to get this game of charades started the way she wanted.

'Good morning, Flynn's Phantasmagorian Emporium of Tea. Dee speaking.'

There was a definite pause on the other end of the phone before a deep male voice replied. *Excellent*. She had put him off his stride and victory was hers.

Shame that when he replied that deep voice was resonant, disgracefully measured, slow and confident. It seemed to vibrate inside her skull so that each syllable was stressed and important.

'That's quite a name. I am impressed. Good morning to you, Miss Flynn.'

The way he pronounced the end of her name was quite delicious. 'I have just made it up, and that's the idea. And how are you feeling this morning, eh? I hope that there is no bruising or delayed mental trauma from your exciting trip to the tea rooms yesterday evening. I wouldn't like to be responsible for any lasting damage.'

She almost caught the sound of a low chuckle before he choked it. 'Not at all,' Sean replied in a voice that was as smooth as the hot chocolate sauce Lottie made to pour over her cream-filled profiteroles.

'Excellent news.' Dee smiled and winked at Lottie, who was leaning against her shoulder so that she could hear every word. 'So, does that mean you have found me a superb replacement venue that will meet my every exacting need?'

'Before I answer that, I have a question for you. Are you free to join me for a breakfast meeting this morning?'

Dee held out the phone and glanced at Lottie, who rolled her eyes with a cheeky grin, stifled a laugh and headed off into the kitchen, leaving Dee to stare at the innocent handset as though it were toxic.

'Breakfast? Ah, thank you, but the bakery opens at six-thirty, so Lottie and I have already had our breakfast.'

'Ah,' he replied in a low voice. 'Misunderstanding. I didn't mean eating breakfast together, delightful as that would be. But it would be useful to have an early morning meeting to go through your list of exhibitors and put a detailed profile together, so that my team can work on the details with the venue you decide on. Pastries and coffee on the house.'

Dee squeezed her eyes tightly shut with embarrassment and mentally kicked the chair.

Sean Beresford had not only made her toss and turn most of the night, worrying about whether the event was going to happen, but apparently those blue-grey eyes had snuck in and robbed her of the one thing that was going to get her through the next two weeks: the ability to think straight.

Of course, a breakfast meeting wasn't about bacon butties and wake-up brews of tea that would stain your teeth. She knew that. Even if she had never been to one in person.

How did he do it? How did he discombobulate her with a few words? Make her feel that she was totally out of her depth in a world that she did not understand?

It was as though he could see through the surface barriers she had built up and see straight through to the awkward teenager in the hot-weather cotton clothes on her first day in a London high school. In November.

She had known from the first second she had stepped inside that narrow off-grey school corridor that she was never going to fit in and that she was going to have to start her life from scratch all over again. She was always going to be the outsider. The nobody. The second best. The girl who had to fight to be taken seriously in anything she did.

But how did Sean see that? Did she have a sign painted in the air above her head?

This had never happened to her before with any man. *Ever*. Normally she just laughed it off and things usually turned out okay in the end.

Usually.

Dee inhaled a deep breath then exhaled slowly. Very slowly.

Focus. She needed to focus on what was needed. That was it. Concentrate on the job. Her entire reputation and future in the tea-selling business was dependent on it. She couldn't let a flash boy in a suit distract her, no matter how much she needed him to make her dream become a reality.

Dee looked out of the tea-room window onto

the busy high street; the first sign of pale winter sunshine filtered through the half-frosted glass. The sleet had stopped in the night and the forecast was for a much brighter day.

Suddenly the urge to feel fresh air on her face and a cool breeze in her hair spiralled through her brain. She quickly glanced at the wall clock above the counter. It was just after nine. Swallowing down her concerns, Dee raised the phone to her mouth.

'I can be available for a briefing meeting. But pastries and coffee? That's blasphemy. Do I need to bring my own emergency supply of tea?'

'Better than that. Following our meeting, I have set up appointments for you at three Beresford hotels this morning. And they all serve tea.'

Dee caught her breath in the back of her throat. Three hotels? Wow. But then her brain caught up with what he was saying. He had set up appointments for *her*. Not *them*.

Oh no. She was not going to let him get away with that trick.

'Ah no, that won't work. You see, I still don't feel that the Beresford management team is fully committed to fixing the problem they have created. It would be so reassuring if one of the directors of the company would act as my personal guide to each of the three venues. In person. Don't you agree, Sean? Now, where shall I meet you?'

CHAPTER FOUR

Tea, glorious tea. A celebration of teas from around the world.

Do you add the milk to your tea? About two-thirds of tea drinkers add the milk to the cup before pouring in the hot tea. Apparently this is an old tradition from the early days of tea drinking, when fine porcelain was being imported from China and the ladies were terrified the hot tea would crack the very expensive fragile china.

From *Flynn's Phantasmagoria of Tea*

Wednesday

DEE STEPPED DOWN from the red London bus and darted under the narrow shelter of the nearest bus stop. The showers that had held off all morning had suddenly appeared to thwart her. Heavy February rain pounded onto the thin plastic shelter above her head in rapid fire and bounced off the pavement of the smart city street in the business area of London.

Typical! Just when she was determined to make a good impression on Sean Beresford and prove that she was totally in control and calling the shots.

She peered out between the pedestrians scurrying for cover until her gaze settled on a very swish glass-plate entrance of an impressive three-storey building directly across the road from her bus stop. The words Beresford Hotel were engraved on a marble portico in large letters.

Well, at least she had found the hotel where Sean had asked her to meet him. Now all she had to do was step inside those pristine glass doors and get past the snooty concierge. Today she was a special guest of the hotel management, so she might be permitted entry.

What nonsense.

She hated that sort of false pretension and snobbery. In India she had met with some of the richest men and women in the land whose ancestors had once ruled a continent. Most of the stunning palaces had been converted into hotels for tourists but they still had class. Real class.

She could handle a few London suits with delusions of grandeur.

Dee took another look and sighed out loud as the rain faded and she could see the exterior more clearly.

This was one part of town she didn't know at all well. Lottie's Cake Shop and Tea Rooms were in smart west London and she rarely went further east than the theatres around Soho and Covent Garden. The financial and banking part of the City of London past St Paul's Cathedral was a mystery to her.

At first sight the outside of the hotel looked so industrial. Metal pipework ran up one side of the wall; the lift was made of glass and looked as though the architects had glued it to the outside of the stone block building.

There was nothing welcoming or friendly about the entrance at all.

Just the opposite, in fact. It was imposing. Cold. Austere. Slippery and grey in the icy rain.

Where was the connection to that warm and communal spirit that came with the ritual of making tea for people to enjoy?

It was precisely the kind of building she avoided

whenever possible. In fact, it gave her the shivers. Or was that the water dripping down onto her jacket from the back of the bus shelter?

Dee closed her eyes and, ignoring the two other ladies waiting at the bus stop, exhaled slowly, bringing her hands down from her cheeks to her sides in one slow, calm, continuous motion.

If there was ever a time to be centred, this was it.

This had been her decision. She was the one who had volunteered to organize the London Festival of Tea. Nobody had forced her to take on all of the admin and co-ordination that came with pulling together dozens of exhibitors, tea growers and tea importers looking for any excuse to show and sell their goods.

But there was one thing that Dee knew for certain.

This was her big chance, and maybe even her only chance, to launch her own business importing tea in bulk from the wonderful tea estates that she knew and understood so well, and the passionate people who ran them.

This was her opportunity to show the small world of the tea trade that Dee Flynn was her father's daughter and had learnt a thing or two after spending the first fifteen years of her life travelling the world from tea plantation to tea plantation. Peter Flynn might have retired from the world of tea importing, but his little girl was right up there, ready to take over and make a name for herself as an importer.

Just because her parents had found out the hard way that there was a big difference between importing tea other growers had produced and running your own tea plantation, it did not mean to say that she was incapable of running a business.

And she was determined to prove it.

Of course, that had been last summer while she'd been working for a big tea-packaging company. Before Lottie had asked her to help her run the tea rooms in her cake shop. Her life had certainly been a lot simpler then.

But she had done it. No backing out. No giving in. No staying put in a nice, safe job in the back room of the tea importers while her so-called boyfriend Josh took the credit for the work she had done.

Josh had been so kind and attentive that her good nature had stepped in the first time he had struggled over a technical report. He really did not have a clue about the tea and had really appreciated her help. For a few months Dee had actually believed that they could have a future together, and the sex had been amazing.

Pity that it had turned out that Josh was waiting for his real girlfriend to come back from her gap year travelling in nice four-star hotels. Walking in on the two of them in bed last August had not been her finest moment.

Past history. Done and dusted. No going back now. And good luck to them both. They were going to need it.

Dee blinked her eyes open and smiled across the street as the rain shower drifted away and she could see patches of blue in the sky above the hotel roof.

Idiot! She was overreacting.

As usual.

This was probably where Sean had his office. There was no way that he could offer her a conference room in a hotel this swanky. This was a five-star hotel for bankers and stockbrokers, not rough and ready tea growers and importers who were likely to drop wet tealeaves on the no-doubt pristine hand-woven carpet.

She was just been silly and she was exhausted from the worry.

Time to find out just what Sean had come up with.

With a quick laugh, Dee shook the rain from the sleeves of her jacket and dashed out onto the pavement in a lull in the traffic as the lights turned to red and the queue of people at the crossing ran across the busy road.

In an instant she was with them, her boots hitting the puddles and taking the splashes, but she made it.

Taking a breath, Dee lifted her chin, chest out, and rolled back her shoulders as she stepped up to the hotel entrance. For the next few hours she would be D S Flynn, tea importer, not Dee from the cake shop.

Stand back and hear me roar.

She flashed a smile at the doorman, who held the heavy glass door open for her, but the frosty look he gave her almost sent her scurrying back outside, where it would be warmer.

With one bound she was inside the impressive

building. Shaking off the rain, she looked up and froze, rocking back on her heels, trying to take in what she was looking at.

White marble flooring. Black marble pillars. Tall white orchids in white ceramic bowls shaped like something from a hospital ward. And, in the centre of the reception area, a large sculpture fabricated from steel wire and white plastic hoops hung from the ceiling like an enormous deformed stalactite.

Well, that was one spot she wouldn't be walking under. If that monstrosity fell on her head, the tea festival would be the least of her problems.

Ha. So the interior *did* match the outside.

The only warmth in this room was the hot air blasting out from vents high in the walls.

Dee gazed around the reception area, from the black leather sofas in the corner to the curved white polymer reception desk.

There was no sign of Sean, but she was five minutes early.

Dee started to stroll over to the reception desk but changed her mind. The rail-thin receptionist with the stretched-back, shiny, straight ponytail and plain black fitted suit was collecting something from a large printer on the other side of the desk and probably had not even noticed her coming in.

It might be more interesting to watch Sean work from this side of the desk. As a hotel guest. People-watching was one of her favourite pastimes. And free!

Dee strode over to a black high-back chair and slid as gracefully as she could onto the narrow seat. The stainless-steel legs were about the same thickness as the heels on some of Lottie's designer shoes and she didn't entirely trust the chair to take her weight.

Comfort had clearly not been one of the design specifications for this place.

She stroked the skirt of her cotton dress down over her warm leggings and neatly clasped her hands in her lap.

A butterfly feeling of nerves fluttered across her stomach and into her throat as the heat from the vents started to blow on her shoulders.

Memories of sitting on a hard bench at a railway station at a tiny Indian stop waiting for her parents to come and collect her flitted through her brain. Those had been the days before mobile phones, and her parents would not have used one even if they could, so all she'd been able to do was sit there and wait with her luggage and presents. And wait, worrying that something had happened to them, alone in the heat and crush of the ladies' waiting room, for long hour after hour before the kindly station master had offered to phone the tea estate for her.

It turned out that her dad had been working on a problem with one of the shipping agents and had forgotten that she was flying back from London to spend Christmas with them and that they had agreed that she should take the train to the nearest station that day.

Work had always come first.

Even for those who loved her best in this world.

It had been two years since she had last seen them. She couldn't afford the air fare when she needed every penny for the tea rooms and they certainly couldn't spare any cash to fly back to see her now they were retired.

But it would have been fun to have them here for the tea festival at a Beresford hotel of all places. They would have found this all very grand, and probably have been a bit intimidated, but she had promised to send them photos of the event and write a long letter telling them how it had gone.

And they certainly would have been impressed with Sean Beresford. Now, there was a man with a good work ethic! Her dad would like that.

With those good looks and all the money he wanted, Sean would have pre-booked dinner-and-drinks dates already scheduled into his electronic diary to share with his no-doubt lovely girlfriend.

In fact that might be her now, at the reception desk. All polished and groomed; pretty and eloquent. A perfect choice for the second in line to the Beresford hotel fortune.

Sean would probably be astonished that Dee had taken the trouble to look him up on the Internet. For research purposes, of course.

It was amazing the amount of celebrity gossip his father Tom and brother Rob featured in, but Sean? Sean was mostly photographed shaking hands with some official or other at the opening ceremony of the newest Beresford hotel.

Perhaps he did have some hidden talents.

Dee shuffled out of her padded jacket and picked up a brochure about the hotel spa treatments. She was just considering having hot rocks placed on

certain parts of a girl's body which were not supposed to have hot rocks on them when there was
a blast of cool air from the front entrance and she
shivered in her thin dress as she turned to see who
had let the cold in.

It was Sean.

Only not the Sean who had sat on her floor the
previous evening. This version of Sean was a different kind of man completely.

He stood just inside the entrance shaking the
water droplets from a long, navy waterproof raincoat—a different one from last night, but just as
elegant. She could tell because the smiling doorman was helping his boss out of his damp coat
and she caught a glimpse of a pale-blue silk lining
with a dark-blue tartan stripe. Very stylish. Classy.
Smart. A perfect match for the man who wore it.

Sean's face was glowing from the cold wind and
rain and he ruffled his hair back with his right
hand like a male fashion model on a photo-shoot.
The master of the ship. Lord of all he surveyed.

He looked taller somehow. More in control. Last
night he had invaded the tea rooms and entered
a foreign territory with strange new customs and
practices. But here and now the difference shone

out. This was his space. His world. His domain. Confidence and authority seemed to emanate out from him like some magical force-field.

No wonder the doorman was happy to take his coat; there was absolutely no mistaking that he was the boss.

She envied him that confidence and physical presence that came from a wealthy family background and the education to match. He had probably never known what it was like to be ignored and sidelined and made to feel second rate. It was as if they were from different worlds.

Sean rolled back his shoulders, picked up his briefcase and strode out towards the reception desk. And as he turned away Dee sucked in the breath that had been frozen in her lungs.

The fine navy cloth of his superbly cut business suit defined the line of his broad shoulders. From the way his legs moved inside those trousers, she wouldn't be in the least bit surprised if Sean made regular use of the gym facilities she had just been reading about in the hotel magazine.

That confident stride matched his voice: rich, confident and so very self-assured of his identity. He knew who he was and liked it.

This version of Sean could have graced the cover of any business magazine. He was the personification of a city boy. A man used to being in authority and calling the shots.

The second son and heir.

A man who would never know what it felt like to have to cash in his pension fund and savings to pay the staff wages.

A lump formed in Dee's throat and she turned her gaze onto what passed for the floral display on the coffee table.

Her sweet, kind father had been too soft-hearted to cut the wages for the estate workers when it had become obvious that his dream tea plantation on Sri Lanka was not able to pay for itself. Those wages paid for health care and made it possible for the workers' children to go to school. How could he take that away from them? How could he be responsible for ruining so many people's lives? But, even when they were selling their possessions, her parents had kept reassuring her that she shouldn't worry, they would get their savings back. It would all work out for the best in the end.

Dee exhaled very, very slowly and focused

on the pattern of the marble floor tiles beneath her boots.

Past history.

And it was not—*not*—going to happen to her.

History was not going to repeat itself.

She was not going to lose her tea shop or let her dream slip away. With her contacts and experience, she had the technical ability to go right to the top. Now all she had to do was make it happen. No matter how scared she was.

She had worked so hard to get to this point, she could not afford to let her foolish pride get in the way.

Even if it meant asking for help now and then.

A rustle of activity across the room broke the hushed silence of the reception area and she looked up just as Sean turned away from the desk and saw her.

There must have been something about her that amused him, because she felt those blue eyes scan her entire body in a flash, from the toes of her practical red boots to the top of her head, before they slid down to her face. His gaze seemed to lock onto hers and stay there, unmoving, as though he was trying to decide about something.

Whatever it was, the corner of his mouth slid into a lazy smile which reached his eyes as they locked with hers and held them tight.

The heat of that smile warmed the air between them faster than the hot-air vent behind her legs.

The few hotel guests and staff milling around disappeared and all Dee could see was the handsome man in a suit and tie standing at the reception desk.

It was as though they were the only people in the room.

Dee had often wondered what it would feel like to be the star of the show and the centre of attention. To have people adore you and admire you because you are so very special.

Well, now she knew.

It felt…wonderful.

Instead of squirming away into a corner out of embarrassment, she stretched her head high and stared right back at Sean.

Her blood was thumping in her veins, filling every cell of her body with confidence and life.

And something else. Because, the longer he smiled at her, the more she recognized that telltale glint of animal attraction in his eyes. Attraction which had nothing to do with the suit and everything to do with the man wearing it.

Elemental. Raw. Alive.

A look that was flicking switches she had locked down into an off position ever since she'd found Josh in bed with a pretty blonde and decided to focus on her career plans and put herself first for once.

How did he do that? How did he make her want to flick her hair, run out to the nearest department store and buy the entire lingerie department and latest beauty products?

Was there an executive training course for that? Or did it come naturally?

One thing was for certain: this hotel was looking better by the minute.

Sean could not resist smiling as he crossed the floor to where Dee was sitting. She was sitting looking up at him with a look of total innocence and sweet charm. As though she had not planned her outfit today with one single purpose in mind: to knock any chance of sensible thought out of his brain.

A printed floral dress above grey leggings which

seemed to have tiny hearts embroidered on them. And her hair? Short, cropped into a pixie style. Textured into a mass of tight brunette curls which any man within a thousand feet would want to run his fingers through and tousle up a bit.

But it was her eyes that captivated him.

Who was he kidding? Those pale-green eyes reached out, grabbed him by the man-parts and tugged him to her with a steel cable that just got tighter and tighter the closer he came.

After Sasha he had set his female-resistance setting on high. But there was something about Dee that was simply irresistible.

She looked like a bright spring flower against the monochrome hotel design scheme. And just as fragile. Slender and small. A greenhouse blossom which could be knocked over in the slightest cold breeze.

No way. This tiny girl was the one who had stopped him falling flat on his face last night. Then had beaten him up verbally.

'Fragile' was not how he would describe her.

Interesting was more like it. Intriguing. Enchanting.

Who was she? Apart from a tea fanatic?

'Good morning, Miss Flynn.' He smiled and stepped forward and held out his hand. 'I am so sorry to have kept you waiting.'

'Actually, I was early,' she replied and her long slender fingers wrapped around his with a firm positive grip before sliding away. 'Couldn't wait to hear what you have lined up for me.'

Completely inappropriate images of what those fingers would feel like on other parts of his body flicked like a video show through Sean's mind and he gave a low cough and took a tighter hold of his briefcase.

He pointed the flat of his right hand towards the office suite. 'I have booked one of the breakout rooms. Shall we?'

'Breakout rooms?' Dee laughed as she got to her feet and flung her coat over one arm. 'That sounds ominous. Is that where your hotel guests organize the escape committee?'

'Just the conference delegates.' Sean smiled. 'And only when they have had enough of the speakers. Most of the business meetings we hold here need separate rooms where they can hold workshops and seminars away from the main group. It works well.'

'Workshops,' Dee repeated and followed him down a wide corridor fitted with an oatmeal carpet. 'Right. I don't think that I shall be needing any of those.'

'Understood.' Sean nodded and held open the white polymer door to the only small meeting room that was available for the next hour on a busy week day. 'After you.'

Her reply was a quick nod as he stood back, waited for her to step inside, then turned and followed her in.

Only Dee could not have taken more than two steps into the room when she whirled around to face him so quickly that he had to lean back slightly to stop her from swinging her bag into his chest.

Her eyes were wild, flashing green and he could see her breathing fast and light, the pulse throbbing in her neck.

They were so close that he could have reached out and touched her face, or fastened up the top button on her cotton dress which was gaping open slightly as it stretched taut from her coat and bag, revealing that same creamy, clear skin that he had seen last night when she'd worn the one-strap jumper.

'Is something wrong?' Sean asked and looked over her shoulder at the perfectly orderly and clean meeting room with its cluster of tables and chairs.

Dee took one step closer and pressed both hands against the front of his shirt. He inhaled a heady mix of bakery sweetness and spice blended with a spicy floral perfume with a touch of musk which surprised him by being so girly. Sweet. Aromatic. Personal.

She smelt wonderful, but when she lifted her head to reply her gaze darted from side to side with alarm and there was just enough of a quiver in her voice for his every nerve to stand to attention.

'There are no windows in this room. Not one. I can't stay here. No way. No how. No discussion. Borderline claustrophobia. Had it for years. Nothing I can do.'

Then she shuddered and his hands automatically reached out and rested on her hips to steady her, hold her, warm her and sooth away whatever problem was causing her such clear distress.

'Sean, I am really sorry, but I hate this hotel. Do you have another one? Because I have to get out of here. Right now.'

CHAPTER FIVE

Tea, glorious tea. A celebration of teas from around the world.
On a cold winter's day? A piping-hot infusion of ginger and lemon will do the trick. Fruit and flower combinations are brilliant at lifting the spirits.

From *Flynn's Phantasmagoria of Tea*

Wednesday

SEAN ALMOST HAD to snatch his raincoat from the hotel doorman before dashing out onto the pavement. But it was worth it, because Dee was still waiting to cross the busy road, her attention focused on shrugging into her duvet jacket, her bag clenched tight between her knees.

'Dee. Wait a moment. What about our meeting?'

Her head swivelled back towards him and she looked from side to side for a moment before she realized who was calling out. Instantly her shoulders seemed to slump and she fastened up her jacket and slung her bag over one shoulder.

'Meeting? Can we do it over the phone? I really don't want to go back inside.'

She shrugged her shoulder bag higher and sighed out loud. 'I think that I've embarrassed myself enough for one morning. Don't you?'

Then she pulled a dark-green and gold knitted cap out of her jacket pocket and pulled it down over her pixie cut. 'Right now I am far more interested in finding the nearest piece of park, grass, garden, anything in fact, that will make me forget the white holding cell that I have just been in. Okay?'

Then she noticed the crossing light had turned green and she turned on the heels of her ankle boots and strode forward, her cotton dress swinging from side to side above the grey-patterned leggings.

Her outfit was the perfect match for her personality: stylish, modern and surprisingly sexy. Just like the woman wearing them. The ankle boots were just short enough to display a finely turned ankle and toned calf muscles.

And just like that his libido switched up another level.

What had he told Rob? That he had missed his two weeks in the sun? Well, maybe he could find some of that life and colour right here in London in the shape of Dee Flynn.

He rarely met women outside work, and never dated guests or his employees, so his social life had been pretty static ever since the disaster with Sasha.

But there was something about this girl that screamed out that her open, friendly manner was real. Genuine. And totally, totally original. Which in his world was a first.

She knew exactly who she was and she knew what she wanted. Yet she was prepared to tell him that she had a problem with closed, windowless spaces and she had to change the rules to deal with it.

Sexy and confident inside her own skin.

And she was totally unaware of how rare a thing that was, especially in the hotel business, where most people had hidden agendas. Her goal was simple: she had placed her trust in the hotel and they had let her down. And she needed him to put that right. Because it was personal. Very personal.

Was that why he had taken time out today to meet her when his conference team were perfectly capable of finding a replacement venue in one of the other Beresford hotels in this city?

She marched ahead, then stopped and looked up at the street names high on the wall of the buildings on either side, hesitant and unsure.

'Looking for somewhere in particular, or will any stretches of grass do?'

Dee whirled around to face him, her eyebrows squeezed together, her hands planted firmly on her hips. 'I have no clue where I am. Seriously. I left my street map back at the shop and was too frazzled to jump on the next bus. I would probably end up even more lost. And shouldn't you be back doing your hotel management thing?'

She waggled her fingers in the direction of the hotel with a dismissive sniff.

'What? And leave my special client lost in a strange part of the city? Tut tut. That would be a terrible dereliction of my duties. Please. Allow me to be your tour guide.'

He closed the gap between them on the narrow pavement outside the smart row of shops and waved his right hand in the air. 'As it happens, I know this area very well even without a map. And you wouldn't want to see me get into trouble with the senior management, would you?'

'Is this all part of the Beresford hotel's five-star service?' She asked with just enough of an uplift in her voice to tell him that she was struggling not to laugh.

'What do you think?' he asked, and was rewarded with a knowing smile before she squeezed her lips together, a faint blush glowing on her neck.

Her gaze scanned his face, hesitant at first, but the longer she looked at him, the more her features seemed to relax and she lifted her chin before replying in a low, soft voice which to his ears was like the rustle of new leaves in the trees that lined the street. The relentless noise of the buses, taxis and road traffic faded away until all he could focus on was the sound of her words. 'I think I would like to see the river. Do you know how to get there?'

Sean nodded, and soon they were walking side

by side along the wide, grey stone pavement that ran along beside the river Thames.

'Okay, what was it that made you hate my hotel so much that we had to dash out into the rain?' Sean asked.

Dee winced. 'Do you really want to know? Because I am famous for being a tad blunt with my opinions when asked questions like that.'

He coughed low in his throat and took a tighter grip on his briefcase. 'I noticed. And, yes, I do want to know.' Then he glanced over at her and gave a small shrug. 'It's my job to keep the guests happy and coming back for more. So fire away; I can take it.'

Dee stopped walking and dropped her head back, eyes closed. Her chest lifted and fell inside her padded jacket a couple of times.

'I'm so glad that the rain stopped. I like rain. Rain is good. Snow too. But cold sleet and grey skies? Not so much.'

Then she opened her eyes and looked up at him. 'What were you like when you were fifteen years old?'

The question rocked Sean a little and he took a second before replying. 'Fifteen? Living in London, going to school then working in the kitchens at my dad's first hotel: loading dishwashers, peeling veg, helping to clean the rooms. My brother and sister did the same. We are a very hands-on family and there was no special treatment for any of us. We had to learn the hotel business from the bottom up. Those were the rules. And why do you want to know that?'

'I was born in north-east India. At a tea plantation where my dad was the general manager. He worked for a big firm of Scottish tea importers who owned most of the tea gardens in that district of Assam. And don't look at me like that. I am simply answering your question the long way round.'

'Are you always so curious about other people's lives?' Sean asked.

'Always, especially when I can see the worry on your face. No doubt you have some terribly important business meeting that you should be attending at this very minute instead of putting up with me. As a matter of interest, how long had you given me in your whizzy electronic diary this morning? Just for future reference?'

Sean lifted both hands in the air and gave a low

chuckle. 'A whole fifty minutes. So we are still on the clock. Please, carry on. Your delightful childhood in sunny India. That must have been very special.'

She grinned, shook her head, then carried on walking. 'You have no idea. Both of my parents were working estate managers so I was left with my nanny and the other kids to run feral across a huge farm most of the time outside school. It was paradise. I only went down with serious diseases twice and grew up speaking more of the many local languages than English. I loved it.'

'When did you leave?'

'We moved four times to different estates in fifteen years and that was tough. But they all had the same problems and my dad had a remarkable talent for turning the businesses around. He seemed to have a knack for dealing with people and helping them with what they needed. Mostly better education for their children and health care.' Then her voice faded away and she looked out over the wide, grey river in a daze. 'They respected him for that. I'm sure of it.'

'Did you come back to England for your education?' Sean asked and stepped closer to avoid a couple of joggers.

Dee stopped and turned back to face him, and her eyebrows squeezed together as she focused on his question. 'Partly. But mainly because the firm promoted my dad to be a tea broker. We came back to London when I was fifteen.' Then she exhaled and blew out hard. 'Total culture shock. I had been here for holidays many times, but living here? Different thing.'

Then she paused and licked her lower lip. 'That was when I realized how much I had taken the outdoor life for granted. Being cooped up in a classroom with only a couple of small windows to let in air and light started to be a real problem, and my schoolwork suffered. I found that the only lessons where I could relax were the cookery and art classes where we were taught in a lovely sunlit studio extension at the back of the school.'

She looked up at him through her eyelashes, which he realized were not black but more of an intense dark brown.

'I was okay there. Big open patio doors. Lots of space. And colour; lots of colour. The gardens were planted out in wonderful displays of flowering shrubs and plants. Tubs and hanging baskets. Planters everywhere.'

Then she pressed her lips together tight. 'In fact, that studio was just about as opposite as you could get to that windowless, airless cube of a white room we have just escaped from.'

She titled her head to one side and blinked. 'Human beings are not supposed to be in spaces like that meeting room of yours. Seriously. What was the designer thinking? Monochrome, hard surfaces. No colour or texture. No living plants. If I was a business person, it would be the last place on the planet where I would want to go to work.'

Then she winced and flashed him a glance. 'Sorry, but you did ask. And I am sure that the bedrooms are very nice and cozy.'

'Actually, they are exactly the same. We market the style as minimalist couture. No pictures on the walls and all-white polymer surfaces and sealed tiling.'

'What about the food?' Dee asked in a low, incredulous voice.

'Micronutrients, hand-harvested seafood and baby organic vegetables. It is very popular with the ladies who lunch.'

'Not the same ladies who come into our tea rooms. Those girls can eat! We are run off our feet keeping up with the demand. But I am starting to get the picture. Oh, Sean! I don't envy you that job. How do you survive? Oh no—I've just had a horrible thought. Wait. Wait just one minute.'

Sean stopped walking and Dee stomped up to him, close enough that she had to look up into his face.

'Please tell me that this other hotel is not the same! I'm not sure that I could stand another minimalist venue. Forget the breakfast meeting. All I want is a replacement venue, Sean.' And she clutched hold of the lapels of his raincoat. 'Somewhere with windows and light and air where people can enjoy tea. Because you have to understand, that's what tea is all about. Having fun and sharing a drink with friends and family. The ceremony and the rituals are optional extras. And you can't do that in a cement basement garage. Please give me some light and space. Is that too much to ask?'

Her bright eyes were shining. Her hands were on his coat, so it made perfect sense for his right hand to rest lightly on her hip.

'As it happens, this hotel is the first one on my

list of options. They have a vacancy a week Saturday and can easily fit the numbers you gave on the booking form.'

He flicked his head over his right shoulder. Dee's stunning green eyes widened in surprise and she took a small gasp of astonishment.

'This was the first of the Beresford luxury five-star hotels. Art deco. Original stained glass. Plenty of natural light, and the conference suite opens up onto the lawns leading down to the river. It's also the same place where I cut my teeth as a junior manager so I think I know it pretty well. And not a minimalist detail in sight. In fact, I would go as far as to say it is old school. So. What do you think?'

'Think? I am too stunned to think. Wow. You can officially consider yourself forgiven.'

And, without asking permission or forgiveness, she leant up on the tips of her shoes and tugged his lapels down towards her so that he was powerless to pull back even if he wanted to.

The quick flutter of her warm breath on his cold cheek happened so fast that, when her soft and warm lips pressed against his skin, the fragile sensation of that tender, sweet kiss was like liquid fire burning her brand onto his skin and in a direct line to his heart.

To Dee it was probably nothing more than a quick, friendly peck on the cheek but when Sean looked into those smiling green eyes he saw his world reflected back at him.

He should have looked away. Made a joke, stepped back and pointed out some of the famous London landmarks that were on the other side of the Thames. But for the first time since Sasha the only thing Sean was interested in was the warm glow and welcome that a pair of captivating green eyes held out to him.

Tantalizing. Alluring. He was held tight in their grasp and that suited him just fine. Forget the cold wind. Forget that they were on a public footpath. Forget that she was a client.

All that he could think about was the red glow on her cheeks, and when she tilted her face to one side the first real smile of the day creased the corners of her mouth and lingered there for a moment before reaching her eyes.

Sean lifted his hand and popped a stray strand of hair back under her knitted hat with one finger. He made sure that the knuckles of that hand traced a feather-light track along cheekbones which were so defined and yet so soft that his skin ached to do it again to make sure that he had not mistaken the sensation.

Instantly her head lifted just a little and those eyes recognized a shift in the electricity in the air between them. It had that same power as the energy bolt he had felt when he first saw her in the hotel, but here it was magnified a hundred times.

It seemed only natural to drop his briefcase to the floor, slip both hands behind the back of Dee's head and cradle her skull. When he bent down and pressed his cheek against her temple, he could feel her breath on his skin, and each breath he took was warmed by the scent of the woman he was holding so close to his chest.

His mouth slid slowly down to her lips, making her take a sharp gasp that told him everything he needed to know.

This was a woman designed for pleasure, and given the chance he wanted to be the one to show her just how good that pleasure could be.

Shame that two cyclists just happened to be speed-racing past them at that very second, laughing loudly, followed by a woman on a mobile phone with a tiny yapping dog on a lead.

Perhaps this was not the place. Dee certainly thought so; she let him go so quickly that he almost overbalanced but held it together by keeping a tighter grip on her waist.

Dee grinned back at him, and suddenly it was as if the sunlight in the break in the clouds above their heads was focused on the genuine warmth of her delight. The grey was gone, replaced by an infectious smile which seemed to reach down inside his very being and twist by several hitches that steel wire of attraction that bound them together.

Irrepressible, fun, real. His sunshine on a grey day.

This was what he wanted. This was what he needed in his life.

This was probably why he stepped back, slid his hand from her hip and held his elbow out towards her.

'May I have the pleasure of being your personal hotel guide on this fine February morning, Miss Flynn?'

Dee looked at his elbow, eyebrows high, as though she was getting ready to give him her very best snarky remark, then flashed him a blushing half-smile.

'Well, if you can stand the scurrilous gossip this will create, I may be prepared to risk it,' she replied and threaded her hand through the crook of his elbow. 'Although, there is something you should know.'

'You have a jealous boyfriend at home who is going to track me down and sort me out if I make a move?' Sean chuckled as they strolled up the path away from the river, Dee leaning slightly into his shoulder because of the height difference.

'Hah! Very amusing. Not a bit. No boyfriend, jealous or otherwise. I am working on my master plan to take over the tea trade one festival at a time. No time for boyfriends; hell, no. They are far too distracting to a lady entrepreneur like myself.'

'Of course. I completely understand. Today Lottie's Cake Shop and Tea Rooms, tomorrow the world. I can see it now. And a great idea for a franchise.'

'I know. But the tea shop is only one of my many talents.' Dee coughed dismissively. 'I was quite serious this morning when I answered the shop phone. The tea-import business is at the very early stages and I am taking my time to think about the name of the company and how to brand myself. So important, don't you agree?'

Sean opened his mouth to answer then looked down at this girl who was capable of rendering him silent.

Then he looked at her again in silence before replying. She was serious. Totally, totally serious.

And his interest in her just ramped up another notch.

'I do agree. The right name and brand are crucial for creating the perfect image for your company. It has to be unique, creative but easy to recall. Not easy. Which is why there are a lot of companies making serious money working for clients who have exactly that problem.'

His reward was a short nod. 'I had a feeling that you would appreciate my business sense, which is why I plan to launch my new company at the tea festival. That way I get the perfect feedback direct from the experts in the trade. It's an ideal opportunity.'

Then she looked up at him with a sly glance.

'Ah. So this is not just about the tea. Now I understand; you are taking a chance. That's quite something. Brave.'

'Daft more like,' she replied and flashed him a light, quizzical glance though her eyelashes. 'As a matter of interest… Were you…planning to make a move? Just curious.'

'Might be. Miss Curious.'

'Not Miss Anything. The name is Dee, but my friends call me Dee.'

Then she bumped her head against his side. 'Dee.'

Sean slid his hand down his side and clasped hold of her fingers. 'My friends call me Sean. Conventional, but I like it.'

'Sean,' she whispered and the sound was carried away in the breeze like the sound of the wind in the trees. 'I like it too.'

He grinned and took a tighter hold of her fingers. 'Let me show you my hotel. Somehow, I think it might be a perfect match. Ready to find out?'

'Prakash! What on earth are you doing here?'

A slim, elegantly dressed man with a Beresford hotel name-pin on his lapel and a lively open smile turned towards them in the foyer of the stunning hotel. But he did not have a chance to reply because Dee squealed and practically pounced on him, pressing her chest against his suit before pecking his cheek.

Then she stood back and covered her mouth with her hand.

'Oh no, you're working here. Sorry, Prakash. Especially since your boss is right here with me. Do you know Sean?'

Sean stepped forward and in an instant scanned the employee name-badge and mentally made the connections.

'Prakash.' He nodded. 'Of course.' They exchanged a hearty handshake. 'Haven't you just graduated from the management academy? I know my father was very impressed with the whole team.'

'Thank you, Mr Beresford. It was tough but I learnt a huge amount.'

'But what are you doing here?' Dee pressed, looking into her friend's startled face as she grabbed his arm. 'Last time I saw you was when we graduated from catering college and you were all set to run your parents' chain of family restaurants.'

Ah. So they'd been at catering college together. That would explain why Prakash Mohna was looking shell-shocked. He was probably terrified that Dee was going to start sharing some scandalous student prank that they had got up to.

As though a hidden sensor in the back of Dee's head had detected that Sean was thinking of her, when she turned his way her face twisted into an expression that screamed out: *go on, say something snarky about students.*

'Actually, I am the new conference manager. Started yesterday,' Prakash blustered.

'Conference manager.' Dee laughed and thumped him on the shoulder. 'That's brilliant news. Because I, Miss Dee Flynn of Flynn's Phantasmagorian Tea Emporium, need a conference room. In a hurry. Sean here—' she flicked her head over her shoulder in his direction '—found out that I had been double-booked at another Beresford hotel. And several hundred tea lovers are going to descend on London looking for a tea festival a week on Saturday. Do you think that you can help me out? Because otherwise we'll be setting up the stall in this gorgeous foyer.'

Her college friend flashed Sean a look of sheer panic before licking his lips and waving down a hallway. 'Why don't we check the booking system and find out?'

'Is it computerized?' Dee winced.

'Well, yes, but we also have the printed booking sheet as back-up,' Prakash replied, obviously confused, then he nodded. 'Don't tell me that you are still a complete technophobe? Dee!'

She held up both hands in protest. 'Not a bit. I have a laptop. Lottie has set it up for me and I run my world-class tea empire from the comforts of my own home. Progress has been made.'

Then she turned and opened her mouth to say something with that glint in her eye which told Sean that she couldn't resist giving him a sly dig, but Sean saw it coming and cut it off.

'Human error caused the double booking at Richmond Square, so we are going to have to convince Dee that our systems can handle it.'

Sean looked up at Prakash who had pressed a finger to his lips as though he was finding the fact that his boss and his pal from catering college were on first-name terms very amusing.

'I checked the system this morning, Prakash, and we had a cancellation which might fit the bill. Why don't I leave you to look after Dee and sort out the details while I take care of some other business? I'll be just over here if you need me.'

Sean looked up from the reception desk as Dee's laughter echoed out across the marble foyer. She was strolling out of the main conference room with her arm looped around Prakash's elbow.

Right now Prakash seemed to be doing a fine job of charming their latest client and keeping her entertained.

Strange that every time he looked up Dee just happened to glance in his direction and then instantly turn away. With just enough of a blush on the back of her neck to tell him she was only too aware that they were sharing the same breathing space.

Sean paused. For a moment there he thought… Yes, he was right. They were chatting away in what sounded like Hindi.

Of course. She had grown up in India. Nevertheless, it was still impressive.

Dee Flynn was certainly an unusual girl. In more ways than one.

He had made a mistake when he'd walked into the cake shop last night and taken her for a baker or shop assistant.

This girl was a self-employed tea entrepreneur who was organizing what sounded like a very impressive festival on her own.

That took some doing.

She couldn't be a lot older than his half-sister Annika, who had grown into a lovely and talented photo-journalist. But when it came to organisation? Not one of her strengths, and Annika was happy to admit that, even to him.

Even their father had been impressed with how the shy little blonde girl had blossomed into a lovely teenager and confident, beautiful woman with straight As, and a first-class honours degree from a famous university under her belt.

It was an education designed to open doors. And it had.

He loved Annika and was the first to admit that she had achieved her success by working as hard as he had to make it happen. Yet he did wonder sometimes how things would have turned out for them all if their father had not been there to pay for the private education, with a solid back-up plan and financial edge to give them the support they needed.

Things might have been different for all of them if his father had not insisted that all of his children should grow up together: same school, same house most weekends and holidays.

Three children with three different mothers living in the same house had not always been easy—especially for his stepmother—and they had fought and bickered and had vicious pillow fights just like any other children. But Tom Beresford had forged them into a family and he had done it through love and making sure that each one of them knew that he would always be there for them. The one constant in each of the children's lives.

For that, he was prepared to forgive his dad's womanising ways. Rob never stopped teasing him that his little brother was letting the side down by staying faithful to every one of the lovely women who had agreed to put up with a light and fun relationship with him while it lasted.

Sean Beresford did not do long-term commitment. He had seen first-hand the fallout from that kind of life when you were working twenty-four-seven, and he was determined to learn from his father's mistakes.

But to succeed on your own? With parents who worked overseas? That took a different skill set.

Dee was definitely a one-off.

Suddenly aware that he had been totally focused on Prakash and Dee, Sean bent his head over the conference-centre booking system and one thing was only too obvious: Prakash was not going to be very busy for the next few weeks. Far from it. Compared to the previous year, bookings over the winter had fallen by over forty per cent and were only picking up now for spring weddings and business meetings. Summer was busy most weeks but the autumn was a disaster.

Something was badly wrong here. The recession had hit some London businesses more than others, and large conferences were a luxury many companies could no longer afford. Events booked a year in advance were regularly being cancelled.

Sean stretched up and ran his fingers along the back of his neck, anxious not to make a fool of himself. But the girl in the flowery cotton dress and leggings distracted him by strolling across through to the other room, totally confident and completely at ease, with Prakash and his assistant making notes as they walked.

Their half-whispered words tickled the back of his neck and Sean yearned to drop everything and join in the conversation instead of focusing on the work.

Well, at least they would have one happy customer.

The conference centre at this luxury hotel was in a different league from the facilities at Beresford Richmond Square, which was designed for large seminar groups. Most of the time companies booked the whole hotel for the event and organized special catering and personalized planning.

That did not happen too often in a hotel this size… Maybe that was something he could look at?

Sean quickly checked the hotel brochure. Conference delegates could have a ten per cent discount if they stayed here. At Richmond Square it was fifty per cent. And he already knew that this hotel was never fully booked. Ever.

Perhaps he should be thanking Dee for giving him an idea.

He looked up as the door to one of the ground-floor meeting rooms opened and a stream of hotel guests walked past him towards the sumptuous buffet he had already spotted being laid out.

Slipping in right behind them, Dee smiled back at him over one shoulder and waltzed into the dining room with Prakash leaving Sean to stare after her. And the way her dress lifted in the air conditioning as her hips swayed as she walked.

Suddenly light-headed, Sean blinked. Food. Now, that was an idea.

Sean stood in silence as the chatting, smiling strangers filled the space his newest client had left in her wake, and watched as Dee looked over her shoulder with a wry smile, shrugged her shoulders, then turned to laugh at something Prakash said, before they were swallowed up by the businessmen who were clearly desperate for brunch after a hard morning.

The last thing he saw was the slight tilt of her head and a flash of floral cotton as she sashayed elegantly away from him. Every movement of every muscle in her body was magnified, as though a searchlight was picking her out in the crowd for him alone.

This was a girl whom he had only met in person for the first time yesterday.

Strange that he was even now reliving the moment when her body had been pressed against his arm.

Strange how he was still standing in the same spot five minutes later, watching the space where she had last stood. Waiting. Just in case he could catch a glimpse of her again.

The prettiest woman in the room.

And a very, very tantalising distraction.

Sean breathed out slowly through his nose and turned away.

Before Sasha, the old Sean would have already flown in his lady and made dinner reservations, or drinks that would stretch out into the evening with a long, slow languorous seduction as a nightcap.

But now? Now long-term relationships were for men who stayed longer in one place than a few days or weeks at most. Men who were willing to commit fully to one woman and mean it.

His gaze flicked up to the place where Dee had just been and lingered there longer than it should have.

They were different people in so many ways, yet there was something about Dee that made him want to know her better. A lot better.

He would love to have the luxury of being able to take personal time in London, but that was impossible if he wanted to get his job done before leaving for Paris. Even if that temptation came in the shape of a tea-mad beauty who was different from any other girl that he had met for a long time.

A cluster of older men in suits burst into the reception area, blasting away his idle thoughts in a powerful rush of financial chatter and cold air.

Sean gave a low cough and straightened his back as he nodded to the guests.

Nothing had changed. The work had to come first.

He owed it to his father and the family who were relying on him to get things back on track. There was no way that he could let them down. Not now. Not ever.

Not after all that his father had done for him. For all of them.

Sean looked up at the screensaver on the computer: *The Beresford Riverside. A Beresford Family Hotel.*

There it was. The Beresford family. His rock when things had collapsed around him when his mother had been taken ill. His rock when his father had remarried but kept the children together, making sure that they all felt loved and cherished.

His family was all he had. And he was not going to let them down.

Dee was a lovely girl and a new client. He had been friendly and gone beyond the call of duty. The last thing either of them needed was a long-distance relationship which was bound to end in heartbreak and tears—at both ends of the telephone. From now on he had to keep his guard.

His family had to come first.

It was time to get back to work.

CHAPTER SIX

Tea, glorious tea. A celebration of teas from around the world.
You can't have a cup of tea without something to go with it: from tiny fairy cakes and English cucumber-and-salmon sandwiches to seafood accompanied by warm green tea in Japan. Tea and food are perfect partners.

From *Flynn's Phantasmagoria of Tea*

Wednesday

DEE GAVE PRAKASH a quick finger-wave and then stood on tiptoe and peered over the top of the frosted glass barrier which separated guests from hotel staff.

Sean was sitting in exactly the same position as she had left him well over an hour ago. A plate with the remains of a sandwich sat next to his keyboard, an empty coffee cup on the other.

'You missed a great meal,' she said, but Sean's

focus did not waver from the computer monitor. 'In fact, I am officially impressed. So much so, that I have just come to a momentous decision.'

He flashed her a quick glance, eyebrows high. And those blue eyes seemed backlit with cobalt and silver. Jewel-bright.

'Okay, Mr B. You win,' Dee whispered in a high musical voice. 'You have pulled out the big guns and wowed me with the most fantastic hotel that I have ever stepped into in my entire life. And the conference suite is light, airy and opens out onto the gorgeous grounds. I am powerless to resist.'

Dee lifted her head and pushed out her chest so that she could make the formal pronouncement with the maximum splendour. 'I accept your offer. The Beresford Riverside *is* going to be the new home of the annual London Tea Festival. Con-gratulations.'

Then she chuckled and gave a little shoulder dance. 'It is actually happening. I can't wait. Can-*not* wait. Just can't. Because this festival is going to be so mega, and everyone is going to have the best time.' Then she clasped her fingers around the top of the barrier and dropped her chin onto the back of her hands so that Sean's desk was practically illuminated by the power of her beaming grin.

Sean replied by sitting back in his swivel chair and peering at her with one side of his mouth twisted up into a smirk. 'Let me guess—Prakash introduced you to the famous Beresford dessert buffet in the atrium restaurant.'

'He did.' Dee grinned then blinked. 'And it is spectacular. But how did you know that?'

He shook his head then pointed the flat of his hand towards her and pulled the trigger with his thumb before sliding forwards again. 'The last time I saw someone so high on sugar and artificial colours was at my sister Annika's fourth birthday party. And I know that you don't drink coffee, so it can't be a caffeine rush. How many of the desserts did you sample?'

Dee pushed out her lower lip. 'It seemed rude not to have a morsel of all of them. And they are so good. Lottie would be in heaven here. In fact, I might insist that she comes back with me and tries them all for research purposes.'

'Better give me some warning in advance so I

can tell the dessert chef to work some overtime,' Sean muttered.

Then he stood up and stretched out his hand over the top of the glass. 'Welcome to the Beresford Riverside, Miss Flynn. We are delighted to have your custom.'

Dee took Sean's hand and gave it a single, firm shake. 'Mega.' She smiled and clutched onto the edge of the conference brochure tight with both hands. 'Righty. Now the room is sorted, we can get started on the rest of the organization.'

'Don't worry about that,' Sean replied and walked around to her side of the barrier. He reached into the breast pocket of his suit jacket, pulled out a business card and held it out towards her. 'Prakash will make sure that you have a great event. I wish you the very best of luck, Dee. If there is anything else you need, please get in touch.'

Dee glanced at the business card, then up into Sean's face, then back at the card.

And just like that, the joyous emotional rush of finding this fabulous venue and knowing that her fears had been unfounded was swept away in one spectacular avalanche that left her bereft and mourning the loss.

This was it.

She was being dismissed. Passed off. Discarded.

So that was how it worked? She'd been given the personal attention and star treatment by one of the Beresford family for just as long as it took to get her booking sorted out. Then she was back in line with all of the other hotel guests. Business as usual. Fuss and bother all sorted out.

She was being discarded as not important enough to invest any more time on.

Just as her parents had been.

She had been forced to stand back and watch her parents lose their tea gardens when the money had run out and the powers that be had refused to wait until the tea could be harvested and sold before pulling the plug.

A one-family tea-growing business had not been a priority customer. Not worth their time. Not worth their money. Not worth spending time to get to know who they were and how they had invested everything they had in that tea garden.

She had been a teenager back then and struggling to cope with the relentless exhaustion of training in a professional kitchen after she'd left catering college, powerless to do anything to help the people she loved most.

Her parents had come through it. They had survived. But their dreams had been shattered and scattered to the winds.

Well, history was definitely not going to repeat itself when it came to her life.

Nope. Not going to happen. Not when she was around.

What made it even worse was that it was Sean who was giving her the big brush-off. What had happened to the man who'd been happy to give her a cuddle only a few hours ago after listening to her life story? Now that same Sean was only too willing to pass her off onto an underling to deal with, so that he could get rid of her and get back to his real job.

No doubt there was some terribly important business meeting that required his attention and he could not possibly waste any more time with the simple matter of a conference booking.

It was such a shame. Because, standing there in his fitted suit, pristine shirt and those cheekbones—lord, those cheekbones—he looked delicious enough to eat with a spoon and a dollop of ice-cream on the side.

Shame or no shame, she recognized the signs only too well. And if he thought for one second that he could get rid of her that easily, he was badly mistaken.

'Oh no,' Dee said in a loud voice which echoed around the reception area, making several of the men in suits glance in their direction. 'Big misunderstanding. I obviously have not made myself clear. No business card; I am not going down that route.'

Then she tilted her head slightly to one side and shrugged before carrying on in a low, more intimate voice, confident that she now had his full attention.

'You screwed up. Big time. So now I have to reprint all of my promotional materials and contact loads of exhibitors to let them know about the new venue. Posters, flyers, postcards to tea merchants and tea fanatics. All have to be done again. Then I have to go back to all of the tea shops and online tea clubs with the new details with only a week or so to go. That's a lot of work to get through, and I have a full-time job at Lottie's.'

She pressed her lips together and shook her head. 'Prakash is a pal, but he does not have the level of authority to spend the cash and resources to make all of those things happen and happen fast. It seems to me to point one way. I am going to need that five-star Beresford service from the man at the top.'

Dee fluttered her eyelashes at his shocked face and there was a certain glint in those blue eyes that was definitely more grey than azure. 'You are not off the hook yet, Mr B. In fact, I would say that this is only the start of the project. Now, here is an idea. Shall we talk though the next steps on the way back to your office? You must be very excited about this opportunity to demonstrate your commitment to customer service. And there is an added bonus: we will be working together even longer! Now, isn't that exciting?'

Sean shrugged into his coat and double-checked the long string of emails before popping his smart phone into his pocket. Apparently the Beresford hotels around the world did not have anything so urgent that he needed to jump on a plane and take off at a minute's notice. So, no excuse. He glanced back towards the conference centre.

Dee was still talking to the scariest office manager in the company, and from the laughter coming out of her office they were getting on like a house on fire.

It was first time he had ever heard Madge laugh.

Almost six feet tall and built like a professional rugby player, his very well-paid, über-efficient and organized manager terrorised the reception areas on a daily basis, ruthlessly checking every guest bill, and even his brother Rob had been known to hide when he heard that Madge was chasing up his expenses.

This was turning out to be one hell of a day of firsts and it was not over yet.

Of course, he had tried to convince Dee that he was already committed to making her event a success.

Sean had introduced Dee to three of the full-time conference organizers who took care of event management, and both of the office admin ladies who provided the VIP business concierge service. They had demonstrated their fax and photocopying equipment; their digital scanners and super-fast laser colour printers; their spreadsheets and floor plans; their menu cards and delegate stationery.

And Dee had smiled, thanked them for their time, promised each of them free tea samples and refused to budge one inch.

In fact, if anything the list of items she had written out in her spidery handwriting on the conference pad she had snatched from his desk was getting longer and longer by the minute.

Madge would sort it out, he had no doubt about that, and he had already asked her to make it her top priority.

But there was no getting away from the fact that Dee Flynn was not a girl who gave up easily.

Sean chuckled low in his throat and shook his head. He could not help but admire her for having the strength to stand up and demand what she believed he owed her.

Problem was, from everything he had seen so far, she had no intention of making his life any easier. At all.

In any way.

Because, every time he looked up and saw her with Prakash or one of the team, his brain automatically retuned to the sound of her musical voice and the way she jiggled her shoulders when she got excited. Which was often.

And when those mesmerising eyes turned his way?

Knockout.

Of course, Dee was not the only reason he found it difficult to settle at the Riverside.

It was always strange coming back to this hotel where he had found out the hard way that washing frying pans and loading dishwashers in a kitchen that could serve four hundred hot meals was not for wimps.

Rob's fault, of course. From the very moment that his older half-brother Rob had announced that he wanted to follow his passion and learn to cook professionally, their father had insisted that he should learn his trade from the bottom up, starting in the hotel kitchens and going to the local catering college. No free rides. No special favours or dispensations from the award-winning chefs the Beresford hotels employed, who had learnt their trade through the classic apprentice system, working their way through gruelling long hours at kitchens run by serious taskmasters.

If that was what his eldest son and heir truly wanted to do, then their father had said he would support Rob all the way. But he was going to have to prove it in a baptism of fire. And, where Rob had gone, his little brother Sean had wanted to follow.

Somewhere in the London house their father had a photograph of Rob in his kitchen whites, standing at a huge stainless-steel sink sharpening a knife on a steel, with his brother Sean at his side scrubbing out a pan as though his life depended on it. Rob could not have been more than nineteen at the time, but he looked so deadly serious. Skinny, unshaven and intense. There were only a few years between them in age but sometimes it felt a lot more.

They had both come a long way since then. A very long way.

The sound of a woman's laugh rang out from the office and his body automatically turned as Dee and Madge strolled down the corridor together.

Now, there was a killer team. Dee was probably five feet and a few inches tall in her boots, but looked tiny compared to Madge, who towered above her in smart heels.

Amazing. Madge even smiled at him after shaking Dee's hand and waving her off as though they were best pals who had known one another for years.

Dee seemed to accept this sort of miraculous behaviour as completely normal, and a few minutes later she had found her jacket and they were outside the hotel and heading for the taxi rank.

Only, before the doorman could hail a black cab, Dee rested her hand on Sean's coat sleeve and asked, 'Do you mind if we walk? The rain has stopped, the sun is coming out and I am so busy in the tea rooms I just know that I'll be cooped up for the rest of the day.'

Sean made a point of checking his wristwatch. 'Only if we go a different route this time. I make it a rule not to go the same way twice if I can avoid it.'

'Fair enough,' Dee replied, shuffling deeper into her jacket. 'And, since you're my tour guide, I shall rely on you completely.'

'You didn't give me a lot of choice,' he muttered, but she heard him well enough.

'You can stop pretending that you are put out by my outrageous request for personal attention.

You love it! And I love your hotel. It is gorgeous. Lucky girl; that's me.'

Sean nodded. 'You were very lucky to find the two-day slot you wanted at this much notice. That is certainly true.' He gestured to a side street and they turned away from the busy street down a two-way road lined with stately white-painted Regency houses. 'But, as a matter of interest, what was your back-up plan in case of some emergency? Your Plan B?'

Dee chuckled and shook her head. 'I didn't have one. There is no Plan B. No rescue mission. No back door. No get-out clause. No security exit.'

Sean blew out hard. 'I don't know whether that is brave or positive thinking.'

'Neither,' she replied with a short laugh. 'I don't have anything left in the piggy bank to pay for a back-up plan. Everything I have is in the tea rooms and this event. And I mean everything. If this festival doesn't bring in a return, I shall be explaining to the bank why they won't be receiving their repayment any time soon. And that is not a conversation I want to have.'

Then she threw her hands in the air with a flourish. 'That's why I was having a mini melt-down last night. But no longer. Problem solved. I only hope that Prakash enjoys his job long enough to stay around.'

'What do you mean?'

'I was only talking to Prakash for a fairly short time, but it's obvious that he feels like a tiny cog in a big machine where nobody knows his name or what he wants from the job. It seems to me that you and your dad and brother have created a training system which is incredibly impersonal and cold.'

Then she paused and twisted one hand into the air. 'Not deliberately. I don't mean that. But you are all so busy.'

Dee gave a small shrug. 'Maybe you could take a few tips from a small business and talk to Prakash and the new graduates one to one, find out what they need. It would make a change from a big, flashy presentation in a huge, impersonal lecture theatre. It might work.'

'That's an incredibly sweet idea, Dee, and maybe it would work in a cake shop, but we have hundreds of trainees. It would take weeks of work to get around all of them and then process the responses. It is simply not doable. I wish it was. But that's business.'

'No, Sean. You can talk to your graduates for days and give the all of the motivational speeches you like but when they are back in their jobs they have to want to do their best work and be inspired by you and your family. Because you motivate them. Not because they feel they have to perform to bring in a pay cheque. Totally different.'

Then Dee shrugged with a casual smile that left him speechless. 'And who would have guessed that your Madge is a total tea addict? And that girl knows her leaves! Only the finest white tea for her. I am impressed. And I hope you don't mind, but I did give her a voucher for a free cream tea if she came to Lottie's.'

'Mind? Why should I mind if you give away free samples?' Sean replied as he dodged a kamikaze cyclist who served around them. 'But you should try our traditional afternoon tea. It is very popular with the guests—and you seemed to enjoy our desserts.'

'Oh, the food would be amazing. That's not the problem. It's the tea you serve.' She winced as though there was an unpleasant odour. 'It's very nice—and I know the warehouse where you buy it from, because I used to work there—but for a five-star hotel? I have to tell you that you have been fobbed off with stale old tea that has been sitting in those boxes for a very long time. It's certainly not up to the standard I expected. Why are you looking at me like that?'

'Fobbed off? Is that what you said?' Sean replied, coming to a dead halt.

'Now, don't get upset. I just thought that I should point it out. For future reference.'

'Anything else you would like to mention?' Sean asked in a voice of disbelief. 'I would hate for all that great free advice to be burning up inside without an outlet. Please; don't hold back. Fire away.'

He ignored her tutting and tugged out his smart phone; his fingers moved over the keys for a second. 'There. The food and beverages director has been alerted to your concerns. And Rob Beresford is not a man who lets standards slip. What?'

Dee was standing looking at him with her mouth half hanging open. 'Wait a minute. Beresford; of course. I never made the connection. Are you talking about the celebrity chef Rob Beresford?

The one who runs that TV programme sorting out rundown restaurants in need of a makeover?'

'One and the same. And it's even worse than that. He is my half-brother. And the man may look laid-back, but underneath that slick exterior he is obsessed with the quality of everything we serve and as sharp as a blade.'

A ping of reply echoed out from the phone. Sean snorted and held the phone out to Dee, who looked at it as if he were offering her a small thermonuclear device. 'I thought that might push his buttons. He needs your mobile number. Expect a call very soon.'

Dee stared at the phone and shook her head very slowly. 'I don't have a mobile phone. Never had one. No clue how to use one.' Then she looked up at Sean and chuckled. 'I could give him the number for the cake shop, but Lottie would probably put the phone down on him thinking it was a prank call. Would email be okay?'

Sean stood in silence for a few seconds.

'No mobile phone?'

She shook her head again. 'I live above the shop and rarely travel. My friends know where I live. No need.'

'Tablet computer? Or some sort of palm top?' She rolled her eyes and mouthed the word 'no'.

Sean took back his phone and fired off a quick message, then laughed out loud when the reply came whizzing back.

'Have I said something to amuse you? My life's mission is now complete,' Dee whispered and looked up and down the street as Sean bent over his phone as though she were not there. Then she spotted something out of the corner of her eye just around the next corner, glanced back once to check that Sean was fully occupied and took off without looking back.

Sean did not even notice that she had walked off until he had exchanged a couple of messages with Rob, who thought that the whole thing had to be one huge practical joke, and couldn't believe that a girl who was willing to criticize his tea supplier didn't have a phone. So he came up with another idea instead.

An idea so outrageous that Sean was sure Dee would turn him down in a flash, but hey, it was worth a try.

'Well, it seems that you were right, it really is your lucky day. I have a rather unusual request from my brother. Rob is flying in on Friday for...Dee?'

Sean turned from side to side.

She had gone. Vanished. Taken off. Left him standing there, talking to himself like an idiot. What was all that about?

The girl was a mirage. A mirage who he knew had not retraced her steps to the hotel—he would have spotted that—so she must have gone ahead.

One more thing to add to his new client's list of credentials: impatient. As well as a technophobe.

Sean strolled down the street, and had only been gone a few minutes when he turned the corner and walked straight into one of the local street markets that were famous in the area. Once a week stallholders selling all kinds of handmade goods, food, clothing, books, ornaments, paintings and everything else they had found in the attic laid out their goods on wooden tables.

A smile crept unbidden across Sean's face.

His mother used to love coming to these markets and he used to spend hours every Saturday trailing behind her as she scoured the stalls for what she called 'treasures'. Her collections: post-cards of London; Victorian hand-painted tiles; antique dolls with porcelain faces; handbags covered with beads and sequins, most of them missing; cupboards-full of old white linen bedding which had always felt cold and scratchy when he was a boy. But to her eyes, glorious items which were simply in need of a good wash and a good home.

Each item had its own story. A silver snuff-box must have been owned by someone important like Sherlock Holmes, while a chipped tin car had once been the treasured toy of a refugee who had been forced to leave everything behind when his family had fled. Just as she had done when she'd escaped persecution when she'd been a small girl, arriving in London with her journalist parents and only a small suitcase between them. Simply glad to be safe from the political persecution from the new regime in their corner of Eastern Europe.

The horror of being forced to flee from your home to avoid arrest was one thing. But to start again and make your life a success in a new country was something special. Sean admired his mother and his grandparents more than he could say. They had taught him that hard work was the only way to make sure that you were never poor or hungry again. To build a legacy that nobody could take away from you.

No wonder his dad had adored her.

His dad usually had been working all hours of the day and night at one or another of the hotels, but if he was home when they got back, carrying their bags of assorted 'treasures', he'd used to laugh like a train and go through every single one and pretend to love it.

Happy days.

Happier days.

Sean inhaled a couple of sharp breaths.

It had been years since he had been to a street market and even longer since he had thought about coming here with his mother as a boy. Most of the time he would much rather have been playing football with his mates from school. But now? Now they were treasured memories.

Long years filled with good times and bad. Hard, physical work had helped to block out the bad. Long years when he'd usually been so exhausted that he collapsed into bed at night without the luxury of dreams.

Not much had changed there. He was still working so hard that sometimes the days just melted together into one huge blur.

When was the last time he had walked any-where? He always caught a black cab or had a limo waiting to take him to some airport. There was no down time. There couldn't be. His work demanded his full attention and he didn't know how to give anything else but his best.

He had paid the price for the hugely successful company expansion.

Only, at moments like this, he wondered if maybe the cost was too high.

Sasha had been the last of a long line of short-term relationships. His friends had stopped calling because there was always some excellent reason why he couldn't make their dinner or meet up for drinks.

All he had left was his family.

Sean stood in silence, overwhelmed by the sights, sounds and smells of the street market, and allowed all of those happy memories to come flooding back.

The sun broke through the clouds and filled the space with light and a little warmth. The birds were singing in the London plane trees which lined the street and, for the first time in months, he felt a sense of contentment well up inside him.

Shockingly new. Depressingly rare.

But for once he did not over-analyze how he felt or push it away.

He simply gave in to the sensation and enjoyed the moment. Each breath of the heady air seemed to invigorate him. The long-standing stiffness in his neck and shoulders simply drifted away. Gone.

He felt engaged and buoyant at the same time.

He shook his head and sighed. Maybe there was something to be said for leaving the hotel now and again.

And he knew precisely who to blame.

The girl who was strolling down between the market stalls, oblivious to the world, a grin on her face and a skip in her steps. Living in the moment and loving it.

Gorgeous, astonishing and totally pushing all of his buttons.

Dee Flynn was turning out to be the best thing that had happened to him in quite a while.

Forget the rules. Forget over-analyzing his schedule and responding to every email that came in. Time to take some of that personal time he was due and had never taken. And he knew who he wanted to share it with.

Dee dropped her head back and felt the sun on her face.

Oh, that felt so good.

Okay, it was a pale imitation of the sun she had grown up with, but right now she would take whatever sun she could get.

'Sunbathing already? Does this mean that you plan to strip off any time soon? Because if you do I can sell tickets and talk up the tea festival at the same time.'

Dee chuckled from deep in her chest.

Sean. His voice was deep, slow and as smooth as fine chocolate. Unmistakable.

She couldn't be angry with this man. Not when the sun was shining and she had a new venue which was ten times more impressive that the Richmond Square hotel—not that she would tell him that, of course.

She lifted her head and turned to face him. And blinked.

Sean was smiling at her with his hands behind his back and a look on his face that made the hairs on the back of her neck stand on end. Tiny alarm bells started to sound inside her head, and as he stepped closer she fought the sudden urge to buy something from the haberdashery stall. Buttons. Ribbons. Anything.

He had something on his mind and she knew before he opened his mouth that it would involve her stepping outside her comfort zone in a serious way.

This must be how antelopes felt before the lion pounced.

'Sorry I spent so long on the phone. Rob had come up with a few ideas about how to make the best use of your advice,' Sean said and then paused.

One more step and he had closed the distance between them, but before she could respond his hand whipped out from behind his back. He was holding the most enormous bunch of tulips that she had ever seen. And he was holding them out towards her.

No—make that bunches. Lipstick-red tulips that called out to be sniffed; yellow tulips still in bud; and her favourite tulip: stripy parrot blossoms in glorious shades of white and red with splashes of orange and flame. All set off by swords of dark-green leaves with pristine, clean-cut edges.

Without a moment's hesitation she clutched the flowers from his fingers and gathered them into her arms and up to her face.

It was spring in a bouquet.

It was heaven.

'I thought that you might like them,' Sean said with a smile in his voice.

She blinked up into his face, and was totally embarrassed to find that she could hardly speak through the closed sore throat that came with the tears that ran down her cheek.

'Hey,' he said in a voice so warm and gentle that it only made her cry more. 'It's okay. If you don't like them, the flower stall has a great selection of daffodils.'

He ran his hand up and down her arm and bent lower to look into her face. His blue eyes showed such concern that she sniffed away her stupid tears and blinked a couple of times.

'I love them. Thank you. It's just that…'

'Yes. Go on,' he replied, his gaze never leaving her face.

'This is the first time anyone has bought me flowers. Ever. And it is a bit overwhelming.'

Sean looked at her with an expression of complete bewilderment. 'Please tell me that you are joking. Never? Not one boyfriend? Impossible.'

'Never.' She nodded, reached into her pocket for a tissue and blew her nose in a most unladylike fashion.

'Well, that is totally unacceptable,' Sean said and stood back up to his full height. 'You've clearly been treated most shamefully and, as one of the many single men who would love to buy you flowers on a regular basis, I apologize for the oversight.'

Then he smiled with a smile that could have melted ice at fifty paces and which reached his eyes before he opened his mouth.

'Perhaps we can help you to feel more appreciated. Are you doing anything this Friday evening?'

Dee reared back a little and tried to reconnect her brain. 'No. I don't think so. Why?'

'Prakash and the other management graduates are meeting the hotel managers at a company dinner on Friday. Rob is flying in from New York and would love to meet you and talk tea.'

Then Sean lifted her hand that was not busy with the flowers, turned it over and ran his lips across the inside of her wrist, sending all chance of sensible thought from her brain.

'And I...' he kissed her wrist again, his hot breath tingling on the tiny hairs on the back of her hand, his gaze never leaving her face '...would love you to be my date for the evening.'

He folded her fingers into her palm but held her hand tight against his coat, forcing her to look into those blue eyes.

And she fell in and drowned.

'Say yes, Dee. You know that you want to. It's going to be a very special night.'

Words were impossible. But somehow she managed a quick nod.

That was all it took, because the next thing she knew she was walking down past the market stall in the afternoon sunshine with one arm full of tulips. And Sean Beresford was holding her hand.

It was turning out to be quite a day.

CHAPTER SEVEN

Tea, glorious tea. A celebration of teas from around the world.
Visualize a hot summer afternoon. Birds are singing and there is a warm breeze on your face. Scones and jam (no wasps allowed) and refreshing, delicious green tea in a floral-pattern china cup. Bliss.

From *Flynn's Phantasmagoria of Tea*

Thursday

'I DON'T UNDERSTAND the panic. So you're going on a date. With a multi-millionaire. To a management dinner, where all the Beresford hotel bosses will be lined up to kiss Sean's father's feet.' Lottie nodded slowly. 'That makes perfect sense to me. There was bound to be some intelligent man out there who could recognize a goddess when he saw one.'

Lottie waggled the plastic spatula she was holding over the bowl of blueberry-muffin batter in front of Dee's floral-print slimline trousers and canary-yellow long-sleeved top. 'Goddess. Obviously.'

Then she went back to folding in the vanilla and almond extracts and extra fresh blueberries for a few seconds before lifting her head and adding, in a dreamy, faraway voice, 'Why, yes, I did know Miss Flynn before she became the tea consultant to the international hotel chains around the world. But we both knew even then that she was destined for greatness. She had that spark, you see. Special. And she still sends me a Christmas card every year from her Caribbean tax haven. Just for old times' sake.'

Dee gave Lottie a squinty look as she packed napkins into the dispensers on the tables. 'Very funny. Laugh all you like. I'm having a screaming panic attack here. See these bags under my eyes? Haven't slept a wink.'

'I'm not laughing, I'm celebrating,' Lottie retorted as she spooned the batter into paper cases in the muffin tin. 'Sean obviously likes a girl who knows what she wants and can stand up for herself. I know these management types from my

old job. They are always looking for something
or someone to give them a buzz. You will be
fine.'

'A buzz?' Dee groaned. 'I am not trained to give
anyone a buzz. Ever. All I know about is tea!'

'Well, for a start that's not totally not true,' Lottie replied as she sprinkled cinnamon and crys-
tallized brown sugar mixed with chopped pecans
over the tops of the muffins. 'Who was the star
of the celebration-cake contest? And your eggs
Benedict are the best. I can only dream of making
a hollandaise sauce that good. Remember what I
told you when I called you at the tea warehouse
and asked if I could buy you lunch? Universities
do not award first-class degrees just for turning
up. If I am going to set up a business with someone, I only work with the best.'

'True. Three first-class degrees in a class of
forty-two.'

'Damn right,' Lottie said as she popped the muffin trays into the oven and set the timer. 'You, me
and Luca Calavardi.' She stood up and pressed a
sugary hand to her chest. 'Oh, my. Now you've
done it. Reminded me about the lovely Luca.'

'Oh, stop. He was fifty-six, happily married

with children and grandchildren, and only came on the course because he was fed up with being a sous chef all his life. That man had forty years of catering experience under his belt and we had four months.'

'All the more reason to feel proud of what we achieved. Right? Sean is a lucky man, and you are going to knock their socks off. You wait and see. And in the meantime…' Lottie grinned and looked over Dee's shoulder as the doorbell chimed. 'We have our first customer of the morning. They will probably want tea and plenty of it. Go to it, girl. Show them what you can do.'

Dee popped the last napkin holder onto the tray with a snort and walked out of the kitchen and into the tea rooms. But, instead of her usual customers, a short man in a biker's jacket with a motorcycle helmet over one arm was standing at the counter.

'Delivery for—' he glanced at the screen of a palm top computer '—Miss D Flynn. Have I got the right address?'

'That's me. You have come to the right place.' Dee smiled and leant on the counter with both elbows. 'What delights do you have in your bag today?'

The courier flashed Dee a withering glance, then dived into his rucksack and pulled out a small package the size of a book which he passed onto the counter. Dee barely had time to scratch her name with the stylus onto the computer screen before he was out of the door.

'And thank you and goodbye to you too,' Dee said as she turned the box from side to side. Too small for tea samples or festival flyers. Too large for a personal letter.

Intriguing.

A small, sharp knife and a whole bag of foam curls later, Dee stood in silence, peering at an oblong box. It was covered in fluorescent-pink gift paper with a dark-blue ribbon tied in an elaborate bow on the top. There was a small pink envelope tucked into the ribbon and she hesitated for a moment before opening it up and reading the note.

With thanks for a lovely morning. Operating instructions are included and my personal number is number one on the list.
Prakash is next.
Have fun.
Sean.

Dee had a suspicion she knew exactly what was inside the gift box but she tugged away the ribbon and peeked inside anyway.

Staring back at her from a whole pack of scary accessories and manuals was a very shiny, very elegant version of the smart phone that Sean had been using yesterday. But with pastel-coloured flowers in shades of pink and cream printed onto the silver cover.

'Oh my,' Lottie whispered over her shoulder. 'Please excuse my drool. Your boy has very good taste in toys. Am I allowed to be jealous?'

Dee shook her head. 'I know. And it would be churlish to send it back. But…I'm not sure how I feel about Sean sending me personal gifts. I've only known him two days.'

'Think of it this way—it gives him pleasure to send you a phone, and you need one to keep in touch with the hotel if you are out and about doing your organizing thing. It's a winner. Go on, have a play.'

Lottie finished drying her hands and pointed to the shiny silver button. 'That's the power button.' Then she stood back and smiled before giving Dee a quick one-armed hug. 'There you are.

He took your photo yesterday when you hit the streets. You look so sweet carrying those tulips.'

Then Lottie gave a quick chuckle. 'Might have guessed. Dee, darling, I hate to state the obvious but that boy is smitten with you. Totally, totally smitten. And, the sooner you get used to the idea that you are being wooed, the better!'

'Wooed! Have you been sniffing the brandy bottles again? I haven't got the time be wooed by a Beresford. I have a tea festival to organize.'

'Wooed. Whether you like it or not. And, actually, I kind of like it. Sean and Dee. Dee and Sean. Oh yes. And that's my oven timer. Have fun with your phone.'

Dee watched Lottie jog back into the kitchen and waited until her back was turned before picking up Sean's note and reading through it again with a silly grin on her face. He had written it himself, using a pen on paper. That must have been a change for him. The man seemed to live for his technology.

Her foolish and very well hidden girly heart leapt a few beats as she scanned down to the photo he had taken when she'd stopped at one of the market stalls to look at the antique silver teapots.

The girl smiling back at her with her arms full of tulips looked happy and pretty.

Was that how Sean saw her? Or as a girl who had a problem with enclosed spaces who could deck him any time of the day or night?

Her finger hovered over the menu button. She was so tempted so call him right there and then and spend five minutes of easy, relaxed chatter like they had enjoyed the day before. Talking about their lives and how much he missed London sometimes, just as she missed warm weather and the mountains.

Two normal people enjoying a sunny winter's morning. Getting to know one another.

How had that happened?

Dee licked her lips and was just about to ring when a group of women swooped in and headed straight towards her. Customers!

Perhaps Lottie was right. Perhaps she was being wooed. Strange how much she rather liked that idea.

Sean looked out over the London skyline from the penthouse apartment at the Beresford hotel Richmond Square and watched the planted arrangements of ferns and grasses thrash about in the winds that buffeted his high-rise balcony.

No spring flowers or tulips here. Not on a cold evening three storeys above the street level where he had strolled with Dee the previous day.

But she was still with him, and not only in a photo on his phone.

No matter where he went in the Beresford Riverside he could almost hear the sound of laughter and easy chatter. Even Madge had smiled as he'd passed her office.

But it was more than that. Sean felt as though he had been infected with the Dee virus which coloured everything he did and made him see it in a new light.

He had spent the day getting to know the new hotel management trainees. They were a great group of young and not so young graduates: bright, keen and eager to learn. The future lifeblood of Beresford hotels.

It had been a pleasure to take them through some of the Beresford training materials, materials written and tested by experts in the hospitality industry and used in the hotels around the world. And yet, the more time he'd spent standing at the front of the minimalist meeting room at Beresford City, working through the elegant presentation materials while the graduates had scribbled away taking notes, the more his brain had reworked what she had said to him.

Was it really the best way to engage with his staff and motivate them?

Frank Evans was not the only hotel manager who had left Beresford hotels in the last twelve months, and they needed to do something different to keep the staff that were crucial to any hotel business. And it was not just the investment the family made in their training and development; it was that precious connection between the manager, his staff and the hotel guests. That kind of connection took years to build up and could transform customer service.

But it had to come from the top.

Perhaps that was that why he had turned off the projector after a couple of hours and herded these intelligent adults out onto the footpath to the Riverside hotel. He'd let them talk and chatter away as they'd walked, and he'd listened.

It was a revelation. A twenty-minute stroll had given him enough material to completely change his view on how to retain these enthusiastic new employees and make them feel engaged and respected.

The rest of the afternoon had been amazing. He had felt a real buzz and everyone in the room had headed back to their hotels exhausted and dizzy with new ideas and bursting with positivity.

He couldn't wait to tell Dee all about it.

He couldn't wait to see Dee and share her laughter. Up close and personal.

Sean flicked open his notebook computer and smiled at the new screensaver he had loaded that morning.

Dee's sweet, warm smile lit up the penthouse. Her green eyes sparkled in the faint spring sunshine under that silly knitted hat as she clasped the red and yellow tulips to her chest.

She was life, energy and drive all in one medium height package.

The kind of girl who would enjoy travelling on rickety old railways, and always be able to find something interesting to do or someone fascinating to talk to when their flight was delayed. Dee was perfectly happy to spend her days serving tea to real people with real lives and real problems.

She was content to work towards her goal with next to nothing in the way of backing or support, making her dream come true by her own hard work.

His mouth curved up into a smile. He hadn't forgotten the hit in his gut the first time that he had looked into those eyes only a couple of days ago. The touch of her hand in his as they'd walked along the London streets like old friends, chatting away.

Sean turned his screen off, got up, walked over to the window and looked out over the city where he had grown up.

Where was his passion? He was a Beresford and proud to be part of the family who meant everything to him. There had hardy been a day in his life when he had not been working on something connected to the hotels.

Sasha had accused him of putting his work before everything else in his life, blaming him for not having time for a relationship.

But she had been wrong. Sasha had never understood that it was not the work that drove him. It was the love for his family, and especially his commitment to his father.

That was the fuel that fed the engine. Not money or power or success. They came with the job.

When his mother had died of cancer a few short months after that first visit to the doctor, he had shut down, blocking out the world, so that he could grieve alone and in silence. His father was the only person who had been able to get through to him and prove that he had a home and a stable base where he was loved unconditionally, no matter what happened or what he chose to do.

The family would be there for him. His father and his half-brother Rob: Team Beresford.

Damn right. His father might have remarried when he'd gone to university, and he had a teenaged sister on the team now, but that had only made it stronger.

So why was his mind filled with images of Dee, her smile, the way her hair curled around her ears and the small brown beauty spot on her chin? The curve of her neck and the way she moved her hands when she talked?

Magic.

Sean ran his hands over his face.

Was it a mistake inviting Dee to the management dinner and introducing her to the family?

Paris was a short train ride from central London and Dee would love it there.

Maybe he could take a chance and add one more person to Team Beresford?

Only this time it would be for totally selfish reasons. *His own.*

Dee locked the front door, turned the lights off one by one and then slowly climbed the stairs to the studio apartment where she lived above the tea rooms.

What a day!

She never thought that she would be complaining about the tea rooms being busy but they had been going flat out. It was as if the rays of sunshine had encouraged half the tea-drinking and cake-eating population of London out of their winter hibernation in time for a huge sale at a local department store. And they all wanted sustenance, and wanted it now.

The breakfast crew had scarcely had time to munch through their paninis and almond croissants before the first round of sales-mad shoppers had arrived, looking for a carb rush before they got down to the serious shopping, and the crush had not stopped since.

Ending with the Thursday evening young mums' club who held their weekly get-together in the tea rooms between seven and nine p.m. while their partners took care of the kids. And those girls could eat!

Lottie had gone into overdrive and a production line of cakes, muffins and scones had been emerging from the tiny kitchen all day. The girl was a baking machine in the shape of a blonde in whites.

And the tea! Lord, the tea: white; green; fruit infusions; Indian extra-strong. Pots. Beakers. And, in one case, a dog dish for a guide dog. She must have hand-washed at least sixty tea cups and saucers by hand because the dishwasher had been way too busy coping with the baking equipment.

They had never stopped.

But there were some compensations.

Whenever she had a moment it only took one quick glance at the huge display of bright tulips which Lottie had moved onto the serving counter to put the smile back on her face. Sean!

Dee padded through the small sitting room into

her bedroom, unbuttoning her top as she went, and collapsed down on her single bed.

She slipped off her espadrilles and dropped her trousers and top into the laundry basket before flopping back onto the bed cover, arms outstretched.

Bliss! The bedroom might be small but Lottie had agreed to a rent which was more than affordable. And it was hers. All hers. No need to share with a nanny or friend or relative, as she'd had to for most of her life growing up. This was her private space and she treasured it.

She bent forwards and was rubbing some life back into her crushed toes when the sound of Indian sitar music echoed around the room and made her almost jump out of her skin.

Dee scrabbled frantically from side to side trying to work out where the song was coming from for a few seconds, before she realized it was bellowing out from the phone that Sean had sent over that morning.

Dee picked it up and peered at it before pressing the most obvious buttons and held it to her ear. 'Hello. This is Dee. And I should have known that you would set my ringtone to something mad.'

'Hello, this is Sean,' a deep, very male voice replied with a smile in his voice. The same male voice that had kept her awake most of the previous night, reliving the way it had felt to saunter down the streets with Sean holding her hand.

Which was so pathetic it was untrue.

It was her choice not to have a boyfriend. And just because he had asked her to be his date at a company dinner did not mean that they were dating. Not real dating. His brother wanted to talk to her about tea. It was a business meeting.

She had tried that line on Lottie, who had still been laughing and muttering something about her being delusional when she'd staggered home.

'I was wondering how you were getting on with your new phone. Do you like it?'

She snuggled back against the headboard and smiled. 'I do like it. It was one of those unexpected gifts that take you by surprise and then make you smile. Thank you. Sorry I haven't had time to call. We have been really busy.'

'No problem. And you can change the ringtone to anything you like. There are several to choose from on the special options menu.'

Dee held the phone at arm's length and made a

scowl before holding it closer. Suddenly she felt as though she was being asked to sit an exam and she had not had time to study the subject.

'Sean. It is flowery and shiny, and there are so many touch-screen buttons that working out which one to use is going to take me the rest of the day. If I can stay awake that long. I'm long past the tired stage.'

'I know what that feels like.' He breathed out hot and fast. Then his voice faded away until he was speaking in little more than a whisper that reached down the phone and sent tendrils of temptation into her mind, mesmerizing, tantalizing and delicious. 'So here is an idea—have dinner with me tonight. I know a few restaurants in your part of town and we can have a great meal and a glass of wine while I squeeze in a master class on how to use your phone.'

Just the way he breathed out the word 'squeeze' was so suggestive that Dee almost dropped her new phone.

Dinner?

Oh, that sounded good.

But she was shattered and full of cake.

And not sure that she could sit opposite Sean

Beresford without pouncing on him, which would be bad news for both of them.

'That sounds great, Sean, but work has been mad and I ate earlier. And now you have made me feel extra guilty for not calling to thank you.'

'No need. This is the first real break that I've taken all day. And if anything I should be thanking you.'

'Why? Talk to me. After all, that's why you sent me this phone. Wasn't it?'

A gentle laugh echoed down the phone that warmed her in places that even her best hot tea could not reach. It was a laugh designed to tantalize any female within earshot and make her skin prickle with awareness. Right down to her toes. Pity that it was a sensation she liked more than she would ever be willing to confess to a man like Sean. He would enjoy that far too much.

'I was giving a presentation to our new group of trainee hotel managers this morning and after thirty minutes in the all-white holding cell, as you described it so delightfully, I began to understand what you meant by an airless, windowless room. So do you know what I did?'

'You went to the park and sat on benches and

fed the ducks.' Dee smiled. 'The wannabe managers had to train the ducks to race for the food
and the trainee with the fastest duck got the best
job in the hotel chain. Was that how it worked?'

'Ah. Duck training and Pooh sticks are only
used in the advanced management courses. These
were first-year students. If it had not been raining,
I might have given them a treasure map to follow around London, but that option was out. So I
decided to take your advice instead and I moved
the whole group to the conservatory room at the
Riverside, opened every door to the lawns and
turned the presentation into a discussion about
hotel design and meeting customer expectations.
It was fascinating. And useful. Every one of those
trainees seemed to come to life in the conservatory. They were transformed from sitting in total
silence to being open and chatty and much more
relaxed. You should have seen their faces when I
told them why we had moved.'

Dee sucked in a breath. 'Did you mention my
name so that they could pin it to a dart board for
target practice?'

'Not specifically.' He laughed. 'You were a val-
ued event planner who gave me feedback on the

repressive feeling of the breakout rooms. But they totally got it, in a way that I couldn't have predicted. Instead of telling them about the impact of room design, they described how they felt in the two spaces and worked it out for themselves. It was brilliant. Thanks.'

'Ah. So that is the real reason for this call. It's confession time. What you really want to say is that you listened to my whining about how intelligent people shouldn't be packed into closed box rooms and then pretended that you had come up with the idea all by yourself. Is that right?'

'Drat, you have seen through my evil plans,' Sean replied in a low, hoarse voice which sent shivers down her back. She imagined him sitting in his office in the minimalist hotel surrounded by all-white marble and smooth, plastic surfaces, and instinctively pulled the silky cover over her legs.

'Are you still at work?' she asked, daring to take the first move.

'I just got back to the penthouse at Richmond Square. The view from up here is fantastic. Pity you aren't here to share it with me. Floor-to-ceiling windows. Breathtaking skyline. I have a feeling you might enjoy it.'

Dee closed her eyes to visualize how that might look and took a couple of breaths before replying. 'Sorry to disappoint you, but I would hate to be one of those girls who only suck up to you because they want to share the view from the penthouse over breakfast.'

The second the words were out of her lips, she winced in embarrassment. What was it about this man that caused apparently random sounds to emerge from her mouth which bypassed the brain?

'You could never disappoint me. And, as it happens, I know how to make breakfast without needing to call for room service.'

I bet you do.

'I told you that you were cheeky.' Dee smiled and nibbled at one corner of her little fingernail. 'But I may have been mistaken about that.'

'So you do make mistakes?' Sean hit right back across the net. 'And just when I thought that you had all of the answers.'

'Cheeky does not come close. Brazen might be a better description. Does this wonderful breakfast include tea?'

'Dee,' he replied in his rich, deep, sensual tone

that reached down the phone and caressed her neck, 'for you, it would include anything you like. Anything at all.'

Suddenly she was glad that she was lying down because her legs seemed to turn to jelly and her throat went dry.

Closing her eyes should have helped but all she could hear was his lazy, slow breathing in her ear which did nothing at all to calm her frazzled brain.

A handsome man who she liked far more than she ought to was holding something out to her on a velvet cushion, gift-wrapped and sumptuous, and she already knew that it would be astonishing.

And terrifying. She was going to have to face him in less than twenty-four hours and somehow she had to get a hold on this out-of-control attraction before it spiralled away into something more elemental which could only ever be a short-term fling.

So she did what she always did when someone came too close. She put a smile in her voice and hit him right back between the eyes.

'Would that be part of the Beresford five-star service or the VIP special?'

His open and carefree laughter was still ringing in her ear when she said, 'Goodnight, Sean. See you tomorrow.' And she pressed the red button then turned the phone off.

Goodnight, Sean. Sleep tight.

CHAPTER EIGHT

Tea, glorious tea. A celebration of teas from around the world.

Finding the perfect tea to drink with your meal is just as tricky as matching food and wine. One tip: green tea flavoured with jasmine is wonderful with Chinese food but serve it weak and in small cups, and add more hot water to the pot as you drink. And no hangover!

From *Flynn's Phantasmagoria of Tea*

Friday

IT WAS ALMOST six on the Friday evening before Dee was finally satisfied that all of the leaf-tea canisters were full, the tea pots were all washed and ready for the Saturday rush and that everything the tea rooms needed for an eight a.m. start was in place.

But she still insisted on helping Lottie load the dishwashers, then cleaned the floor and generally got in the way of the last-minute customers, until Lottie had to physically grab her shoulders and plop her into a chair with a steaming cup of chamomile until the closed sign was up on the door.

Whipping away her apron, Lottie poured a cup of Assam and collapsed down opposite Dee with a low, long sigh before stretching out her legs.

Her fingers wrapped around the china cup and Lottie inhaled the aroma before taking a sip. Her shoulders instantly dropped several inches.

'Oh, I am so ready for this. When did Fridays get so mad?'

'When you decided to have a two-for-one offer on afternoon cream teas, that's when. I have never served so much Indian tea in one session. How many batches of scones did you end up making?'

Lottie snorted. 'Six. And four extra coffee-and-walnut cakes, and three chocolate. And I gave up counting the sandwiches. But the good news is… it worked. The till is full of loot which I will be taking to the bank before the lovely Sean picks up his princess to take her to the ball.'

'The ball? I'm not so sure that I would call a management dinner a "ball". But the food should be good and apparently all the Beresford clan will be there en masse to toast the staff. So there's a fair chance I will score a free glass of fizz.'

Lottie cradled the cup in both hands and sat back in her chair. 'Ah. So that's what the problem is,' she said, then blew on her tea before taking a long sip. 'For the next few hours you are going to be up close and personal with Sean's father and his swanky brother and sister, and you're feeling the pressure. I see.'

'Pressure? I don't know what you mean. Just because his dad founded a huge chain of luxury hotels, and Sean's older brother, Rob the celebrity chef, is flying in from New York especially for the occasion, it doesn't mean that the family will be snooty and look down their noses at me.' Dee flashed a glance at Lottie. 'Does it?'

'No, not at all. Why should they? And if my experience of management meetings is anything to go by, the owners will be way too busy talking to the staff and making sure they feel the love to worry about extra guests.'

Then Lottie leant her elbows on the table and grinned. 'Think of it this way—you are going to a great night out in a lovely hotel on the arm of a handsome prince. You are a goddess! What can possibly go wrong?'

Dee choked on the tea that went down the wrong way and had to grab a couple of napkins to stop her from spraying Lottie with chamomile through her nose.

'Are you kidding me?' she spluttered. 'I have a long list of things that could go wrong, and the more I think about it the more opportunities I have to put my foot in it. Everything from what I am going to wear, which is a nightmare, right through to my total inability to control the words that spill out of my mouth.'

Her hands came up and made circles in the air. 'And, when it does all go wrong, I can wave good-bye to my free conference centre and any chance I have of finding a replacement venue at this short notice for the tea festival and—' she swallowed '—show Sean up at the same time. Now, isn't that something to look forward to?'

She slid her cup out of the way and dropped her head forward until it rested on the table. 'I am doomed.'

Lottie shook her head and smiled. 'What rubbish. Do you remember that first day we met in catering college? I had come straight out of the business world, had no clue what to expect and turned up to the first morning wearing a designer skirt-suit, four-inch heels and a silk blouse. I thought that the first morning would be paperwork and class schedules, just like university. Instead of which, I spent the whole day gutting fish and making white sauces.'

Dee put her head to one side and sniffed. 'It was a different look, I'll give you that.'

'So you said—right before you passed me your new chef's coat and trousers.'

'I had spares. You hadn't,' Dee replied, sitting up, her shoulders slumped. 'The funniest thing was when you had them bleached and starched at some posh dry cleaners overnight. It was hilarious.'

'It was kind of you to offer me them in the first place. Which is why it is time for me to return the favour. I cannot believe I am saying this, because I think all your clothes are brilliant and suit you perfectly, but if you're worried about not having a cocktail dress to impress Sean's family then I can probably help you out.'

'You're going to lend me one of your fancy

posh frocks?' Dee asked in a quiet voice, eye-brows high.

Lottie nodded her head. Just once.

Dee propped her chin up with one finger and looked up at Lottie through her long, brown eye-lashes.

'And the shoes and bag to match?'

'Natch!' Her friend slurped down the last of her tea and rolled her shoulders back. 'Good thing we take the same shoe size. Come on; we have a lot to do and not much time to do it in. You, my girl, are going to take time out and celebrate just how much you've achieved whether you like it or not. Let the makeover begin.'

An hour later Dee paced up and down on the bedroom carpet in bare feet, her hands on her hips as she moved from her bed to the wardrobe, then back to the bottom of her bed again.

It was quiet in her bedroom. A chilly, gentle breeze fluttered the edge of the heavy curtains, bringing with it the welcome sound of chatter and traffic from the street below. The sound of nor-mal people living normal Friday-evening lives.

But inside the room the atmosphere was any-thing but calm.

She stretched out her hand to lift the black fitted cocktail dress from the hanger, then froze. *Again.*

She blinked at the dress hanging on the wardrobe door for several seconds, nodded, then slipped her feet into Lottie's favourite stiletto-heeled sandals and tried a few tenuous steps. Lottie had told her that she should practise walking in them in case she had to take the stairs in the hotel. Four-inch heels with a platform slab under the toes were going to take some getting used to.

Two steps. Three. Then her right foot toppled over sideways on the slippery couture leather and she had to grab hold of the wardrobe door before she almost twisted her ankle as it bent over.

These were not shoes! They were instruments of torture, which had clearly been designed by men who hated their mothers and were determined to make all women suffer as a result. That was the only possible explanation!

And it did not matter one bit if they had pristine red soles if she couldn't walk in them.

Her shoulders slumped and she rested her forehead on the waxed oak panel, not caring that she might destroy the make-up which had taken Lottie an hour to put on, wipe off, then put on again in a different way.

She was terrified that she was sending out the wrong message. Or was it the right message?

She had been aiming for elegant and attractive, while the girl who stared back at her from the mirror looked like a stranger. Some clone from a fashion magazine. Not her. Not Dee Flynn, the wannabe tea merchant.

This wasn't working.

She had been mad even to think that she was ready to go out on a date with Sean Beresford. Even if it was for only one evening.

She tottered to her bed in one shoe, fell backwards and let her arms dangle over the sides.

She was just about to make herself a laughing stock in exchange for a few canapés and a glass of fizz in a luxury hotel.

Dee bit down on the inside of her lip. Deep inside, where she kept her dreams and most sacred wishes, she knew that she had every right to stride into that hotel in these high-heeled shoes with her head high and stun the lot of them, including Sean. Strong, and confident that she was the equal of anyone there.

She had worked for this success and deserved to be treated like a goddess.

Drat Sean for reminding her that she still had a long way to go.

Dee closed her eyes, her throat burning and tears stinging at the sides of her eyes.

She was pathetic.

This handsome and attentive man had chosen her to be his date for the evening. Which was so amazing that she still couldn't believe it.

The past few days had passed in a blur of activity and mad work.

Sean had kept his word, and Prakash and Madge were now her official best friends in the whole world. Nothing was too much trouble. Extra power points for the hot-water heaters? No problem. Portable kitchen equipment, refrigerators and study tables appeared out of nowhere like magic.

Apparently the word had come down from on high that, whatever Miss Flynn needed for her festival of tea, the team had to make sure happened.

Especially when the boss, the one and only Mr Sean Beresford, had seemed to find his way into the conference area several times during the day, just to make sure that everything was on track.

Oh, it was on track. *In more ways than one.*

Strange how many times in the day he'd found a way to brush against her hand with his, or look over her shoulder at some suddenly vital piece of information on the floor plan.

She'd had to stop the tickling, of course. That had got completely out of hand and she'd had to scold him about being professional in front of his staff.

Of course, he had insisted on regular tea breaks. Just the two of them, sitting around an elegant table in the hotel dining room, chatting about her critique of the quite good tea the hotel served. And all the while he'd told her anecdotes about his work in the hotel trade which had her clutching her stomach with laughter, and family stories about the antics his brother and sisters got up to.

And maybe it was just as well that she had been kept busy. It had kept her mind from mulling over all of those intimate moments they had shared since he had walked into the tea rooms: the sly glances that set her pulse racing and the gentle touch of his hand on her back or arm. His kindness. His quiet compassion. His humour.

A girl could fall for a man like that.

Hell. She was already halfway there.

Then her smile faded. This evening was turning into a date with Sean when she should be focusing on taking her dream one step closer to being a reality.

And that sent a cold shiver across her shoulders.

She couldn't let the exhibitors down. Some of the tea merchants were coming a long way to show London what tea was all about.

And she couldn't let Sean down either.

No wonder she had the jitters.

Dee stole another glance at the dress hanging outside the wardrobe.

Lottie had done a fantastic job and the girl in the mirror looked every bit the type of sophisticated, elegant girl that Sean was used to having on his arm.

It was the world that Lottie had been born into. A world of luxury and privilege where eating dinner in a Beresford hotel costing hundreds of pounds was something her family did without thinking.

Lottie had her own problems to deal with, no doubt about that, but she could never truly understand what it felt like always to have been the new girl with the second-hand school uniform and the strange accent. Never feeling as though she fitted in. No matter what she did to change her clothes, her hair and the way she spoke, she was always going to be different. And her parents had loved that about her. Loved that she was unique.

Pity that as a teenaged girl going to a city high school the last thing the fifteen-year-old Dee Flynn had wanted to be was unique.

Strange. She thought that she had conquered that particular battle years ago when her flair for catering had taken her higher than she had ever expected.

But that was not the only reason for the jitters.

For the next few hours she would be dealing with Sean's father and his wife Ava, their daughter Annika and Sean's older brother Robert—the professional celebrity chef and current pin-up for a lot of trainee chefs at catering college. And Sean— the blue-eyed boy who had come to her rescue.

How was she going to make polite chit chat with Sean when they had become…what? Event planners? Friends? Or as close to it as you could be when you had spent half the week together.

Dee wrapped her arms around her bare waist,

squeezed her eyes tightly shut and relived, once more, the sensuous pleasure of his gentle kiss in the park and the touch of his hand on the small of her back. All of those subtle moments where she had felt him next to her.

No matter that those thoughts had made for very little sleep the night before. In an hour or so she would be seeing him again. Holding him. Just being in the same room within touching distance.

Delicious.

Her eyes flicked half-open and she glanced across at the brightly coloured tulips which she had popped into a plain white milk-jug on her desk. She could smell their fragrance anywhere in the room, and just seeing the blossoms reminded her of Sean all over again.

His laugh. His smile. The expression of pure pleasure and delight on his face when he'd telephoned his brother the other day and talked to her about his family. They truly were the most precious people in the world to him. He loved his family. And they loved him right back.

It would be so special to be on the receiving end of that kind of devotion.

Had it only been a few days since Sean had

walked into the tea room? It felt so much longer. And like the tulips he would fade and go out of her life. Back to his hotel chain, bottomless wallet and first-class everything. Back to the life she would never have.

A low groan of exasperation escaped her lips, and she would have wiped her eyes but Lottie had just spent her evening using make-up brushes Dee had not known existed to create the face that she was wearing. She dared not mess it up.

She dared not mess any of this evening up.

Too much was at stake. The tea festival was serious business and people were relying on her to do the very best she could.

But why now? Of all the times she could have chosen to have a crush, why did it have to be now, and why, oh why, did it have to be on Sean Beresford—the big-city hotel executive with the shiny, shiny lifestyle and looks to die for? The man who was in line to run the Paris branch of the Beresford hotel empire?

Fate had certainly played her a blinder of a hand. And Sean was currently holding all of the aces.

Sean could make her laugh like no other man, and discombobulate her with equal ease. But she dared not tell him. Could not tell him. Letting him know how attracted she was would only lead to heartbreak, disaster and embarrassment on both sides. He had his life and she had hers, and never the twain would meet. Wasn't that how the poem went?

One evening—that was their deal. Sean had kept his side of the bargain. Now it was time for her to keep hers.

Shame it was so hard to remember that fact when he was so close.

She smiled and slipped off the bed.

Maybe Lottie was right—maybe it was time to celebrate everything that she had achieved and take time out to enjoy herself.

Why shouldn't she enjoy his company for this evening? He had asked her to be his date. And that was precisely what she was going to be.

His date. Yes. That was it. Tonight Sean would be her date who she could rely on not to let her down. Even if it did mean never letting him out of her sight.

Sean rang the doorbell of Lottie's Cake Shop and Tea Rooms. Twice. And heard the bell tinkle inside the shop.

There was a bustle of movement from behind the front door and he could see a dark shape slip forward; as he lifted his chin, the ornate half-glass door opened inwards.

A woman dressed in black was standing just a few feet away: slender, medium height and absolutely stunning.

So stunning that he had to do a double take for his brain to recognise who was standing in the doorway smiling at him with a quizzical look on her face.

It was Dee Flynn. Only not the hard working, tea-obsessed version of Dee he had half the week with.

She had been transformed into a completely different person.

This Dee was dressed in a black cocktail dress: sleeveless, with a high collar tied behind her neck with a ribbon. And a low-cut back. Totally hot.

Sean had seen enough French couture dresses, and had bought enough fashion for Sasha and Annika to know the real thing when he saw it.

The dress fitted her perfectly, the fabric draped close to her waist then flaring out over the slim hips to just above the knees.

Sheer black stockings covered long, slim but muscular legs.

Silk shoes with heels so high that for the first time during the week she came almost to his height.

In a flash he could suddenly feel the life force of this woman emanate towards him, and her energy sparkled like the jewels in the gold bracelet on her wrist. Intoxicating, invigorating and bursting with confidence.

She was effervescent, hot and so attractive he had to fight down that fizz of testosterone that clenched the muscles under his dress shirt and set his heart racing just at the sight of her.

'Hello,' he said, suddenly keen to break the silence and stop the ogling. 'I thought it might be safer to stand outside just in case you had your judo costume stashed behind the counter. Last time I barely made it out alive.' Then he grinned. 'You look amazing, by the way.'

'Why, thank you. You don't look too bad yourself.' She nodded with her head towards the counter. 'Do you want to come in out of the cold? I just need a minute to get my coat.'

'No problem; we have plenty of time. No need to

rush.' He smiled and followed her into the warmth of the tea rooms. He was happy to be able to spend a few extra minutes alone with Dee before they joined the noisy crush of hotel guests and the management team, who were probably just hitting the bar back at the hotel.

Dee smiled back at him then swivelled towards the back of the room. Then, as he watched in horror, she flung both of her arms out into the air and launched herself towards the counter, as her right foot twisted over sideways and the girl literally fell off her shoe.

Sean leapt forward and grabbed her arm so that she wouldn't fall, and heard her slow hiss of pain as she winced and exhaled sharply.

'Are you okay?' he asked, looking into her face in concern.

Her response was an exasperated sigh followed by a sharp nod. 'Fine. Just dandy. My ankle will survive. Unlike my dignity.'

Then she turned her back on him, feeling stupid and humiliated, and scrabbled to slip the silly shoe back onto her foot and fasten the strap tighter. But her trembling fingers let her down and the shoe fell to the floor.

Before Dee could reach down to scoop it up, she sensed his presence seconds before a strong hand slid onto each side of her waist, holding her firm. Secure.

She breathed in a heady fragrance of fresh citrus aftershave and testosterone that was all Sean, which made it impossible for her to resist as he moved closer behind her until she could feel the length of his body from chest to groin pressed against her back.

His arms wrapped tighter around her waist, the fingers pressing oh, so gently into her rib cage and Dee closed her eyes, her pulse racing. It had been a long time. And he smelt fabulous. Felt fabulous.

Sean pressed his head into the side of her neck, his light stubble grazing against her skin, and her head dropped back slightly so that it was resting on his.

Bad head.

Bad heart.

Bad need for contact with his man.

Bad, full-stop.

One of his hands slid up the side of her dress and smoothed her hair away from her face so that he could press his lips against the back of her neck.

'Is there a rule somewhere that dictates that lovely ladies lose all sensible parts of their brain at the sight of shoes they can't actually walk in? Because it does seem to be a very common affliction. I see it everywhere I go. Sad, really.'

Dee tried to pretend that it was perfectly normal to have a conversation with her back pressed against the pristine dinner suit of the most handsome and desirable man she had ever met.

'Absolutely,' she whispered. 'They belong to Lottie, and she promised me that these were the latest thing in limo shoes. Dancing was out unless I wanted permanent disfigurement, but standing in one place could work. Would you mind holding me up here a little longer? I have a small problem standing up straight in Lottie's stilettos and talking at the same time, and you might not be there to break my fall when I try to make it as far as the car.'

He chuckled deep in his chest as though suppressing a smile, and the sound reverberated across her collarbone, down her spine and into regions which were previously closed to reverberations of any kind.

Sean continued to breathe into her neck, and

one of his hands slid up from her waist to move in small circles on her shoulder. The room began to heat up at a remarkably rapid rate.

She clasped hold of the serving counter as Sean gently, slowly, slowly, slid down the length of her body until he could reach down and pick the sandal from the floor.

It was quite remarkable that he also needed to touch the inside of her leg with his fingertips as he did so, sending shivers up and down her spine, which made it seriously difficult to breathe, focus and talk at the same time.

'Over the years I have been dragged by the ladies in my family around every fashion shop and footwear retailer in London at one time or another so I could carry their loot home. And we never, ever, bought shoes which they didn't try on in the shop and at least totter a few steps in. Walking any distance—now, that was different.'

She slowly lifted one of Sean's hands from her waist, and pushed gently away from him, instantly sorry that she had broken the touch, but Sean had other ideas and held her even tighter this time as she turned to face him.

Without her shoes, her head came up to his chest

and she leant back against the counter so that she could look into the smiling, quizzical, handsome face of a truly nice man.

His eyes never blinked or left hers, and her breathing seemed to match his; it was a few seconds before he broke the silence.

'Did I mention that I am a hotel manager? Yes? I did? Well, we have these terribly practical health and safety standards which mean that I cannot condone any footwear which is likely to lead to personal injury. Not in our hotels.'

He took a step back and held both of her arms out wide as his gaze stayed locked onto her wonky feet.

He flicked one hand in the air and tutted. 'My hands are tied. No choice—you can either slip your shoes off and go barefoot the whole evening, or you pop back inside and change into something you can walk in and stand in for several hours. What's it to be?'

CHAPTER NINE

Tea, glorious tea. A celebration of teas from around the world.
The tea a person chooses to drink for pleasure is as unique as their fingerprint. Personal and special. And a true insight into their character.

From *Flynn's Phantasmagoria of Tea*

'I HOPE THAT you are not going to inspect the contents of my entire wardrobe,' Dee snorted as Sean bounded up the stairs from the tea shop to her apartment and followed her along the narrow corridor. 'Because I'm going to tell you now that my selection of footwear suitable for a conference dinner is rather limited.'

'Not at all.' Sean smiled, enjoying the view as Dee skipped up the stairs in front of him and trying not to ogle too blatantly. The memory of her judo training was still too fresh to forget in a hurry. 'Your delightful choice of clothing has been inspired this week and I expect nothing less.'

Dee came to a dead stop outside a white-painted door and he held onto the bannister as she looked down at him with something close to nervousness in her eyes.

'What is it?' he asked with a smile. 'Worried that I will reveal the terrors of your boudoir to the world?' He pressed his right hand to his chest, lifted his head and said in a clear voice, 'As a true gentleman, I promise that your secrets are safe with me.'

Dee lifted both eyebrows high. 'No doubt. But that's not the problem. It's just that—' she coughed and Sean caught a shy blush at the base of her neck '—Lottie is the only person who has seen my bedroom before, and I am actually quite shy about showing my space to other people. In fact, I think it might be better if you wait downstairs. I shouldn't be too long.'

Sean shook his head very slowly. 'Not a chance. I'm not going anywhere.'

Dee sighed and folded her arms. 'Has anyone ever told you that you are annoyingly stubborn?'

'Frequently. It is one of my finer qualities,' he

replied in a light, lilting voice. 'Once I make my mind up about how to do something or a particular plan—that's it. My plans are not for changing.'

She gazed at him for a few seconds before slowly unfolding her arms.

'This tea festival has a lot to answer for,' Sean heard her mutter, but she turned and opened her bedroom door, swinging her shoes in one hand.

Sean stood at the door and took a breath as he tried to take in what he was looking at.

For a small bedroom Dee had managed to squeeze in a wide pale-wood wardrobe and a table under the window. An upright bookcase stacked with papers, magazines and books of all sizes took up the rest of the wall as far as her bedside cabinet.

The walls had been painted in a warm shade of cream. All of the soft furnishings in the room were variations of shades of lavender and primrose yellow, including a cream quilted bed-cover embroidered with tiny blossoms.

The whole room was calm, orderly, clean, serene and tranquil. Feminine without being over-the-top girly or pretty. It was the type of colour scheme and arrangement several of his interior designers had introduced for the new boutique-hotel range his sister was running.

Sean realized with a shock that it was the exact opposite of what he had been expecting. Shame on him for making judgements about the choices Dee would make in her home. Shame on him for judging her. Full-stop.

A smile crept up on him unannounced.

Dee Flynn was turning out to be one of the most astonishing people that he had ever met.

'You can come in if you promise not to touch anything or criticize,' Dee said as she lifted a silk kimono from the bed, swung open her wardrobe door and pulled out a hanger.

'Thank you. This is…a lovely room.'

She coughed and whirled around to face him.

'Don't sound so surprised. What exactly were you expecting? Did you think I had made a nest of straw from old wooden tea chests or something?'

Sean held up both hands. 'Not a bit. I simply didn't think that you would go for a Scandinavian colour scheme with an English twist. Most of your clothes seem bright and Far Eastern. I thought you might have chosen an ethnic style—something bright. That's all.'

'Ah, you were expecting to see rainbow colours and dark wood. I see what you mean. This must be really quite shocking. But you forget that this is where I come to relax at the end of the day. I need this quiet space to help me centre myself and calm down and focus. Otherwise, I think I really would go nuts with the chaos that is my daily life.'

'Well, I know what that feels like. Especially with jet lag,' Sean replied and squeezed past her and picked up a silver-framed photograph from her computer desk.

A tall, slender, grey-haired man in white tunic and trousers was standing with one hand resting on a wooden balcony, the other hand across the shoulders of a dark-haired woman wearing a bright azure top and wrap skirt. All around them was exuberant green foliage, and a riot of flowering plants of all shapes and colours spilled out from pots and planters.

'Are these your parents?' he asked, and gestured with his head towards the photo.

Dee put down a shoe box and came and stood next to him.

'Yup. That's Mum and Dad on the veranda of the house they are renting in Sri Lanka. They love it there and I certainly cannot see them coming back to the UK now that they are both retired, especially in winter. The lifestyle is so different for retired people in a hot climate. And they can make their pension go a long way.'

'Do you see them often?'

'Once a year I save up for a flight and set up some appointments at the tea plantations. It's an amazing treat, and tax deductible. Actually, the owner of the estate where my folks live will be at the tea festival next week. It will be nice to see him again, even if he is a tough negotiator when it comes to his best tea. Mum and Dad get on with him and he treats the estate workers very well.'

'So you only see them once a year? That must be tough. Do they have Internet?'

She threw back her head and laughed out loud. 'Oh please, don't make me laugh. It took Lottie an hour to put this make-up on and she will go mad if I wipe it all off. But in answer to your question...' she dabbed the corner of her eyes with a tissue '...my folks are anti-technology in a big way. That place they are renting has a generator which breaks down at regular intervals but they get by without it most of the time. So, no—no Internet, computer, mobile phone or anything close to what they think is the curse of western culture. But they do write lovely letters. And for that I am thankful.'

Then she paused. 'And I'm talking way too much and not looking for shoes and we have a deadline. Righty; how about these?'

Dee turned and was about to dive into the shoe-box when Sean stepped closer and took a gentle hold of both of her arms and smiled. 'I would much rather listen to you talking about your parents all evening than face the trainee managers. My seminar on time management and productivity can wait until tomorrow. Because right now I have a much more pressing task. I owe you a huge apology, Miss Flynn.'

She cleared her throat and stared back at him wide-eyed. And blinked. Twice. Then waited in silence for him to finish.

'When I fell into the tea shop the other evening and you decked me so delightfully, I filed you neatly away into a box labelled "sexy baker lady" who was responsible for my undignified first view of the tea rooms sitting on my butt. Ah;

don't tut at me like that, because as it happens my view has changed.'

He flashed her a quick wink. 'Not about the sexy— that's still up there—but I was temporarily blinded by the force of your exuberance into thinking that you might be exactly what you appear to be.'

Sean shook his head, looked around the bedroom and exhaled slowly as he moved his head from side to side. 'Wrong. A thousand times wrong. Every day this week you have turned up to work wearing a riot of colour and pattern which has livened up my life and that of everyone you have met. But I am starting to see that that is only one tiny part of who you are.'

Then he stepped closer, then closer still, until he was totally inside her personal space, their bodies almost touching, tantalizingly close. So close that there was scarcely enough room for his hands to slide lightly onto her hips.

'You fascinate me, Dee Flynn. How many sides to you are there? And, more importantly, why are you keeping them hidden? Tell me, because I would really love to know.'

'Why do I wear bright clothing? That's easy,

Sean. It's human nature to judge a book by its cover. You look at the clothes people are wearing and you make an instant judgement about who they are and what they do and where they fit in this crazy world. Especially in Britain, where the class system rules whether we like it or not.'

Her gaze scanned his body from head to toe.

'Look at you—you go to work in a smart suit and shiny black shoes every day. I've never seen you in jeans and a T-shirt. Perhaps you don't own those things. Perhaps this is who you are. And that's fine. You own that suit; it's gorgeous. And it's your job.'

Dee gave a small shrug. 'But the rest of us? The rest of us are doing the best we can to build bridges with people and make connections. I designed most of my day clothes, and they are friendly, open and welcoming for when I am working in the tea rooms. I love wearing them and it gives me pleasure. Practical too. They fit my personality. They express who I am. They are honest and real.'

'So why are you wearing black this evening?'

Dee slid out of his arms, paced over to the window and drew back the curtain so that the cool night air played on her bare arms.

'Isn't it obvious, Sean?'

'Not to me. Talk to me, Dee. Why black?'

She seemed to hesitate for a few seconds before whirling back towards him, and he was shocked to see tears in the corners of her glistening eyes.

'I didn't want to show you up. There; that's it. Happy now?'

Each word hit him right between the eyes like a high-velocity ice cube that melted the second it reached his heart, which burned hot and angry.

No other woman had ever done that for him.

Wanted that for him.

She was not wearing this lovely couture outfit to impress the big cheeses—she was wearing it so that she did not embarrass him.

And it blew him away.

Sean ran his fingers along the slippery silk fabric of her silk kimono strewn on the bedcover. For once in his life, words were impossible.

He slipped his dinner jacket onto the back of the small desk-chair and took a second before turning back to face his amazing woman.

'Not many people surprise me, Dee,' he managed to say. 'Not after a lifetime working in the hotel trade.'

Then he smiled and tapped the end of her nose with his forefinger. 'You don't need a little black dress to make you feel special. You could wear an old bath towel and still be gorgeous. Look at you. No, don't pull away like that. I think that it's time that you saw yourself through my eyes.'

'What are you doing? We're going to be late,' Dee protested.

'Then we are going to be late. You are more important than a room full of hotel management any day of the week. Okay? Besides, you have already pointed out that I have that stubborn streak, remember? I am not leaving this room until you have changed out of this dress and put on something which you love. Something you have chosen. Something you feel wonderful and special in. Then I might help you to choose the shoes.'

'You want me to change? Into what? This dress was really expensive. I don't have anything in my wardrobe to match it.'

'I didn't ask for an expensive dress to keep me company this evening. I asked you—Dervla Skylark Flynn. Not some designer clone. In fact, here is a challenge. What's the one outfit you possess which is the exact opposite of a black designer dress? Come on, you must have one.'

She snorted and shook her head. 'You mean my sari? I can't wear that to a hotel dinner when all of your clan will be there.'

'Yes.' He smiled. 'You can.' And then he bit down on his lower lip and stepped in closer. So close that his chest was pressed against hers as he held her tight around the waist with both hands flat on her back.

'But first we have to get you out of this dress. And, since I am the one who is insisting on it, I feel that it is my duty to help you.' His lips brushed lightly across her forehead. 'Every...' he moved onto her temple '...inch...' then her neck, nuzzling into the space below her ear with his cheek '...of the way.'

Dee closed her eyes and revelled in the glorious sensation of his cheek against hers, the feeling of his hot breath on her neck, the gentle friction of his hair on her ear. Whatever cologne or aftershave he was wearing should have been labelled with a hazard code and stored away in a bomb-proof box, because her sensitive nose and palate were overwhelmed with the rich, aromatic aroma blended with a base note that was nothing to do with a chemical laboratory and everything to do with the man who was wearing it.

Of course, she could feel the sensation of his fingers moving on her back but pressed so tight against his body it was suddenly irrelevant—the only thing that mattered was Sean and this moment they were together. Future. Past. Nothing else mattered but this moment. It was glorious.

So when he slowly, slowly inched his head away from her it was a shock. She eased open her eyes to find that his breathing was as fast as hers and she could see the pulse of the blood in the vein in his neck. Those blue eyes were wide, and the pupils startling deep and dark pools. Dark water so deep that she knew that she could dive into them and never find the bottom.

The intensity of that look was almost over-whelming and so mesmerizing that she could not break away.

No other man had ever looked at her like this before but she recognized it for what it was, and her heart sang. *It was desire.*

Seduction burned in Sean's eyes. Hot and passionate and all-consuming.

His desire for her.

And it astonished her.

Astonished her so much that she forgot to be scared of all of the chaos that love, desire and passion could bring and focused on the joy instead.

He wanted her.

He wanted her badly.

And the huge red switch marked 'danger' that had been buried under a lifetime of disappointment and making do with second-hand love suddenly and instantly flicked up and turned green.

She wanted him right back. On her single bed. And wearing Lottie's posh frock. Forget slow, she wanted fast. She wanted it all and she wanted it now.

It was almost a relief to turn in the circle of his arms so that she could not feel the burning heat of his intense gaze scorching her face.

But that was nothing compared to what she saw when she opened her eyes fully.

She was standing in front of her full-length bedroom mirror on the wardrobe door with Sean standing behind her.

Instinctively she lifted both hands and pressed them to her chest as Sean slid Lottie's black dress away from her shoulders on each side. He had unzipped it as she enjoyed him. Now it was free and all that was holding it up, and protecting her modesty, were her two hands.

Dee stared at the girl in the mirror. Her hair was messed up, her eyes and skin glowing, and there was a handsome man with tight curled brown hair kissing her naked neck and, oh lord, her shoulders.

It was getting very hard to breathe but she could not look away, dared not look away, from the view in the mirror.

Sean was looking at the back of her neck as though it was the most beautiful and fascinating thing that he had ever seen, his fingertips stroking her skin from the innermost curve of her neck and along her collarbone. She could feel the heat from his touch, and the sensation of those fingertips was almost too much for her to tolerate.

A shiver of delicious excitement ran across her back and she saw Sean smile back at her in the mirror.

Lottie Rosemount had a lot to answer for. The mocha lace bra and shorts-style pants she was wearing had been a Christmas present from her, but not even the lovely Lottie could have anticipated that they would be on display in this way when Dee had slipped into them straight out of the shower only an hour earlier.

Slowly Sean brought his hands to the front, laid them over hers and whispered in her right ear in a voice that she could have spread on hot crumpets.

'I want you to see yourself the way I see you. You don't need the dress.'

Dee smiled back at the man in the mirror as he slowly unfurled one finger at a time until only her palms were holding the couture dress against her bra.

'Do you trust me, Dee?'

Speech was impossible but she hesitated. This was it. If she wanted a way out, this was the time to say something or do something to take back control. Instead of which her head lifted and fell in a simple yes, and she was rewarded by a truly filthy grin.

And just like that she grinned back and pulled her hands away so that the dress fell to the floor in a heap around her feet.

She would have bent down to pick it up but that

would have meant bending down while Sean was still holding her tight around the waist.

Bad idea! Such a bad idea!

So instead she swallowed down a sea of doubt and looked back at the mirror and the girl who was standing there in her underwear, with Sean's arms around her waist and his chin resting on her shoulder.

'Tell me what you see,' he whispered.

Her head dropped back and she half-closed her eyes, surrendering her entire body to his hands as they moved in firm and gentle circles in a delicious blissful movement.

Dee dared to open her eyes and watch the scene in the mirror.

Sean stroked and caressed her breasts through the flimsy fabric of her bra, lifting up her left breast then the right. He was slow and gentle, as though he was not in the slightest rush and they had all night to explore one another's bodies.

She felt Sean unclip her bra but did nothing to stop him and leaned back against him, feeling her bare skin on the crisp, white dinner shirt and not caring that she was probably creasing it.

The window was still slightly open and the

chilly breeze wafted in, making her nipples stand proud inside her bra, pushing against the lace.

Sean noticed. She could see his reaction, feel the rise and fall of his chest and the pressure against her back from his trousers.

But instead of going for her nipples the pads of his soft fingertips expertly stroked down from her collarbone down over the top of her cleavage, as though he knew instinctively that was the most sensitive part of her neck.

Then her breasts. Exposed to the air, the dark skin around her nipples was already raised and ready. His fingers stroked all along the length of the side of her breast, moving into a more circular pressure, but then he looked up into the mirror.

But then his fingers paused, and every inch of her skin screamed out for release as he wrapped his arms around her waist and rested his chin on her shoulder so that they were both staring into the mirror at the same time.

'We need to be somewhere. And I need to get some air. Cold air.'

He pressed his lips to her throat and grinned. 'The sacrifices I make for my family. Oh yes...'

And with one last, long, shuddering sigh he slipped back, picked up his jacket and walked slowly out of the bedroom.

CHAPTER TEN

Tea, glorious tea. A celebration of teas from around the world.

Tea is a natural product, hand-picked and completely free from artificial colours and preservatives, but rich in minerals and anti-oxidants. And best of all? Calorie-free.

Perfect for when you need to slip into that little black dress.

From *Flynn's Phantasmagoria of Tea*

Friday

SEAN SAUNTERED CASUALLY into the white marble reception area of the most prestigious Beresford hotel in London, the flashguns lighting up his back.

He might be the youngest director in the family firm but this was the one time a year he was willing to put his Armani tux on show for the press and wear his family pride on his sleeve.

Glancing around the room, he gave a quick wave to the management training team who were already lining up the latest graduates to chat to his father, who was greeting the hundred or so specially invited guests in person, same as always.

Tom Beresford. Straight-backed, tall, dark and impressive. The poster boy for every self-made multi-millionaire who had learnt his trade the hard way. The company PR machine loved to repeat the story about the boy who had started work at fourteen, washing dishes in the kitchens where his mother was the head chef, his father serving in the army overseas. His wages had been a hot meal every day and enough cash to pay his bus fare to school.

The weird thing was, it was all true. Except for one thing: he had been thirteen when he'd started, and barely tall enough to stand at the sinks, but had told the hotel he was older to get the work.

By eighteen he'd been working for the hotel and studying at college and at twenty-one had his first job as deputy manager. The rest was history.

Of course, the PR experts did not go into quite so much detail when it came to his father's complicated personal life, which was way more tab-loid fodder than inspirational reading for young managers. He had certainly enjoyed female company as a single man—and when he was not so single.

Not that he could get away with that now. His lovely third wife Ava had been by his side night after night for the past eighteen years, just as she was greeting the guests tonight, and Sean knew that his father adored her.

He was still the man who had read him bedtime stories every night all dressed up in his dinner suit before heading to the hotel to work.

'Hey, handsome. Feeling lonely?'

Sean laughed out loud as his teenage half-sister Annika hooked her arm around his elbow and leant closer to give him a hug.

He replied by lifting the back of her hand to his lips then glancing up and down her gorgeous aqua cocktail dress. 'Why look at you, pretty girl. All grown up and everything.'

He was rewarded with a soft kiss on the cheek.

'Charmer! But you scrub up nicely. New suit?'

'Had it for months. All ready for the Paris job. New dress?'

'Had it a day.' She sniffed and looked around. 'What have you done with Dee? I noticed that fabulous sari she was wearing when she came in with Rob and then she seemed to disappear. You were very brave, letting him escort your lady friend. Rob is a scamp.'

Then Annika's voice faded away and she gave a small cough. 'Oh my. I think I think you'd better go to the rescue. Don't you? See you later.' And with that she released his hand to move to the cluster of new arrivals who had packed the reception area behind him.

Sean followed the direction of Annika's gaze and stood there, chuckling.

Judging by the number of people clustered around the buffet table, there was obviously something exciting going on. Sean could see Rob's head in the crowd but Dee had emerged from the tea rooms wearing far more practical flat gold sandals. Practical, but it also meant that in a room of tall men she was the orchid shaded by the tall trees.

Except that this was one girl who would always stand out in a crowd.

Especially when she was wearing a gold silk sari, gold jewellery and an azure-and-gold bodice which revealed a tantalizing band of the same taut skin he had admired back in the bedroom.

She took his breath away.

This was no clone. This was a real woman showing that she could act the part when she needed to, and revealing yet another side to her personality that he could never have imagined existed.

He had spent the week learning about one side of Dee Flynn. The woman who had taken a risk with her friend and transformed a simple patisserie into something spectacular. Doing what she loved to do, capitalizing on her passion. On her own terms.

When had he last met a woman like that? Not often. Maybe never. Oh, he had met plenty of glossy-haired girls with high IQs who had claimed they were doing what they truly loved, but so few people knew what they wanted in their twenties that it was astonishingly rare.

He had known precisely what he wanted from the first day he'd walked into his dad's hotel. His career path had been as clear as a printed map. He was going to do exactly what his father had done, start at the bottom and work his way up, even if he was the son of the owner of the hotel chain.

Dee Flynn had done the same.

Maybe that was why he connected with the tiny woman he was looking at now.

They were different from other people.

Different and special.

He was in awe, and ready to admit that to anyone.

Sean stood in silence as the chatting, smiling men and women in business suits who worked for his family filled the space that separated them. But his gaze was locked on one person. And it was not Rob, who seemed to be holding court.

He could hear his brother's familiar roar of laughter warm the room, but Sean's ears were tuned only to Dee's sweet laugh which was like a hot shower.

His senses were razor-sharp. And, as the cluster broke up, he caught sight of her.

She was looking around the room. Looking for him.

She winked at him with a wry smile, shrugged her shoulders and then turned to laugh at something Rob said before they were swallowed up by the trainees and older managers enjoying the delicious food and drink, only too happy to meet the celebrity chef Rob Beresford in person.

The last thing he saw was the slight tilt of her head and a flash of gold silk as she sashayed elegantly away from him.

Dervla Flynn was turning out to be one of the most remarkable women he had ever met in his life, and the last ten minutes had only served to increase his admiration.

He was totally in awe.

Then she slipped out of view as Rob and the whole entourage joined his father in the dining area, leaving him alone with his thoughts.

Strange that he was even now reliving that moment when her body had been pressed against his arm.

Strange how he was still standing in the same spot five minutes later, watching the space where she had last stood. Waiting. Just in case he could catch a glimpse of her again, the most beautiful woman in the room.

For that he was prepared to wait a very long time.

* * *

It seemed like ten minutes had gone by, but when the sitar music sang out from the mobile phone in her embroidered bag Dee was shocked to see that she had been swept up with Rob and his dad, talking food and drink, for over an hour.

There was a text message on the screen:

Ready to escape the noise and crush and get some air? Meet you at the elevator in five minutes. Sean

Sean! She had been so engrossed that she had only spent ten minutes with her date the whole evening. Quickly gathering up her skirts, Dee excused herself and skipped up the steps, and instantly caught sight of Sean, who was beckoning to her.

In a moment he had drawn her into the lift and pressed a card into a slot on the lift button before giving her a quick hug.

'Do you remember that penthouse suite I was trying to talk you into? Well, I seem to recall that this hotel has a private penthouse worth seeing. If you are willing to risk it?'

'Risk it?'

'It's the eighteenth floor, which means a quick trip inside a lift,' he whispered, and grinned at her shocked reaction. 'But it does have a balcony.'

And what a balcony!

Dee stepped out onto a long, tiled terrace, and what she saw in front of her took her breath away.

The rain had cleared to leave a star-kissed, cool evening. And stretched out, in every direction, was London. Her city. Dressed and lit, bright, shiny and sparking with street lamps, advertisements and the lights from homes and offices.

It was like something from a movie or a wonderful painting. A moment so special that Dee knew instinctively that she would never forget it.

She grasped hold of the railing and looked out over London, her heart soaring, all doubt forgotten in the exuberant joy of the view.

It was almost a shock to feel a warm arm wrap a coat around her shoulders and she turned sideways to face Sean with a grin, clutching onto his sleeve.

'Have you seen this? It's astonishing. I love it.' Dee breathed.

'I know. I can see it on your face.'

Then he moved closer to her on the balcony, his left hand just touching the outstretched fingers of her right hand.

But Sean was looking up at the stars.

'Last February it was snowy and cloudy for the whole of the three weeks that I was back in London. But tonight? Tonight is perfect.'

'This is amazing. I had no idea that you could see skies like this in London. I thought the light pollution would block out the stars.'

And she followed his gaze just in time to see a shooting star streak across the sky directly above their heads, and then another, smaller this time, then another.

'A meteor shower. *Sean! Look!*'

'What is it, Dee?' he asked, his mouth somewhere in the vicinity of her hair. 'Have you made a wish on a shooting star? What does your heart yearn to do that you haven't done yet?'

'Me? Oh, I had such great plans when I was a teenager and the whole world seemed to be an open door to whatever I wanted. My parents loved their work, and I was so happy for them when they decided to retire and run their own tea gardens. Warmth. Sunshine. They could not have been happier.'

She wrapped her arms tight around her body. 'But then the hard reality of running a business in a recession where tea prices are falling hit. And they lost it. They lost everything they had dreamt of. And it was so hard to see them in pain, Sean. So very hard.'

'But they stayed. Didn't they?'

She nodded. 'They won't come back unless they have to and if they did… It would break them. And that is what scares me.'

She lifted her head and rested it on Sean's chest. 'I know that I am in a different place in my life, and there are lots more opportunities out there for me, but do you know what? I am not so very different from my folks. I want my own business so badly and I don't know how I could cope if my dream fell apart. Six months ago I was working for a big tea importer and going to night school to study business most evenings and weekends. But Lottie changed that when she asked me to join her in the tea rooms. The time seemed so right. I have volunteered to run the festival and I felt ready to do anything.'

'You are ready. I know it.'

She looked up into his smiling face but stayed inside the warm circle of his arms.

'How do you know what your limits are?'

'You don't. The only way to find out is by testing yourself. You would be astounded at what you are capable of. And if you don't succeed you learn from your mistakes and do what you have to do to get back up and try again until you can prove to yourself that you can do it. And then you keep on doing that over and over again.'

'No matter how many times you fall down and hurt yourself?'

'That's right. You've got it.'

Dee turned slightly away from Sean and looked out towards the horizon, suddenly needing to get some distance, some air between them. What he was describing was so hard, so difficult and so familiar. He could never know how many times she had forced herself to smile after someone had let her down, or when she had been ridiculed or humiliated.

Dee blinked back tears and pulled the collar of his jacket up around her ears while she fought to gain control of her voice. 'Some of us lesser mortals have been knocked down so many times that it is hard to bounce back up again, Sean. Very hard. Can you understand that?'

Sean replied by wrapping his long arms around her body in a warm embrace so tender that Dee surrendered to a moment of joy and pressed her head against his chest, inhaling his delicious scent as her body shared his warmth.

His hands made lazy circles on her back in silence for a few minutes until he spoke, the words reverberating inside his chest into her head. 'Better than you think. Working in the family business is not all fun. I have been in these hotels all my life one way or another. And I still have a lot to learn.'

Dee shuffled back from him, laughed in a choked voice and then pressed both hands against his chest as she replied with a broken smile.

'So that makes two of us who are stuck in the family trade. Am I right?'

'Absolutely. How about a suggestion instead? I know a couple of venture-capital guys who have money to invest in new business ideas. All I have to do is make a few phone calls and… What? What now?'

'I don't want to carry any debt. No maxed-out credit cards; no business loans; no venture capital investment. That's how my dad got into so much trouble and there is no way that I am going there. So thank you, but no. I might be hard up, but I have made some rules for myself. I have already maxed out my credit on my share of the tea shop. I can't handle any more debt.'

Sean inhaled very slowly and watched Dee struggle with her thoughts, her dilemma played out in the tension on her face.

She was as proud as anyone he had ever met. Including himself. Which was quite something.

And just like that the connection he had sensed between them from the moment he had laid eyes on her in the tea rooms kicked up a couple of notches.

And every warning bell in his body started screaming 'danger!' so loudly that in the end he could not ignore it any longer. And he pulled away from her.

She shivered in the cool air, fracturing the moment, and he grabbed her hand and jogged back across the balcony. Sean slid open the patio doors and wrapped his arm around her waist, hugging her to him, the luxurious warmth from the penthouse warming their backs.

'Oh, that's better. Won't you get into trouble with the boss for wasting heat? Oh—you are the boss! Well, in that case, carry on.'

'We should be getting back to the others,' Sean whispered, only his voice sounded low and way too unconvincing. 'They might be missing us.'

She must have thought so too, because she took a last step and closed the distance between them and pressed the palms of both of her hands flat against the front of his white dinner shirt. He could feel the warmth of her fingertips through the fine fabric as she spread her fingers out in wide arcs; the light perfume enclosed them.

'This has been a magical evening. Thank you for inviting me,' she whispered.

Every muscle in his body tensed as she moved closer and pressed her body against his, one hand reaching in to the small of his back and the other still pressed gently against his shirt. He tried to shift but she shifted with him, her body fitting perfectly against his, her cheek resting on his lapel as though they were dancing to music which only she could hear.

So he did the only thing he could.

He kissed her.

She lifted her head and her hair brushed his chin as she pressed tentative kisses onto his collarbone and neck. Her mouth was soft and moist and totally, totally captivating.

With each kiss she stepped closer until her hips beneath the sari were pressed against his and the pressure made him groan.

'Dee,' he hissed, reaching for her shoulders to draw her away. But somehow he was sliding his hands up into her hair instead, holding her head and tilting her face towards him. Then he was kissing her, his tongue in her mouth, her taste surrounding him.

He stroked her tongue with his and traced her lower lip before sucking on it gently. She made a small sound and angled her head to give him more access.

She tasted so sweet, so amazing. So giving.

She gazed at him with eyes filled with such delight, as if she was expecting some suggestive comment about the fact that this penthouse came with a king-sized bed...

And that look hit him hard.

He did not just want Dee to be his stand-in date for tonight. He wanted to see her again, be with her again. He wanted to know what she looked like when she had just made love. He wanted to find out what gave her pleasure in bed, and then make sure that he delivered precisely what the lady ordered.

She was as proud and independent as he was. And just as unforgiving with anyone who dared to offer her charity or their pity.

By some fluke, some strange quirk of fate, he had met a woman who truly did understand him more than Sasha had ever done. And that was beyond a miracle.

Could he take a chance and show her how special she was? And put his heart on the line at the same time?

He slid a hand down her back to cup her backside, holding her against him as he flexed his hips forward, and one hand still in her hair. She shuddered as he slid his hand in slow circles up from her back to her waist, running his hands up and down her skin which was like warm silk, so smooth and perfect. He ducked his head and kissed her again, his hands teasing all the while until he was almost holding her upright.

When their lips parted, Dee was panting just as hard as he was. She looked so beautiful, standing there with her gold sari brilliant against the night sky, her cheeks flushed pink and the most stunning smile on her face.

His response was to wrap his arms around her back and, holding her tight against him, rested his chin on her top of her hair.

Eyes closed, they stood locked together until he could feel her heart settle down to a steady beat.

All doubt was cast aside. Her heart beat for him, as his heart beat for her.

Dee moved in his arms and he looked down into her face as she smiled up at him, not just with her sweet mouth but with eyes so bright, fun and joyous that his heart sang just to look at them. And it was as though every good thing that he had ever done had come together into one moment in time.

And his heart melted. Just like that.

For a girl who was just about as different from him and his life as it was possible to be.

And for a girl who had made her tiny flat the size of the hotel's luggage store into a home and was willing to share her joy with him. And who wanted nothing in return but a chance to see a meteor shower from a penthouse balcony.

God, he admired her for that…. Admired her?

Sean stopped, his body frozen and his mind spinning.

He didn't just admire Dee, he was falling for her.

Just when he thought that he had finally worked out that he had nothing to give to any woman in the way of a relationship.

Think! He had to think. He could not allow his emotions to get the better of him.

If he cared for her at all then he should stop right now, because the last thing Dee needed was a one-night stand which would leave her with nothing but more reasons to doubt her judgement.

He wouldn't do that to her. Hell, he wouldn't do that to himself. It would only be setting them up for heartbreak down the road.

'I think we might want to rethink the whole getting back in time for dessert…' She grinned as though she had read his mind.

'Right as always,' he replied, and stroked her

cheek with one finger. 'God, you are beautiful. Do you know that?'

Dee blushed from cheek to neck. It was so endearing that he laughed out loud, slid his arms down to her waist and stepped back, even though his body was screaming for him to do something crazy. Like wipe everything off the dining-room table and find out what came next.

He sucked in a breath.

'You are not so bad yourself. I had no idea that hotel managers were so interested in astronomy.' And then she bit down on her lower lip and flashed him a coquettish grin. 'Or did I just get lucky? You are one of a kind, Sean.'

Lucky? He thought of the long days and nights he had spent working for the company to the exclusion of everything else in his life, including the girls who had cared about him. Sasha had lasted the longest.

He had sacrificed everything for the family hotel chain. Everything.

Now as he looked at Dee he thought about what lay ahead, and the hard, cold truth of his situation emptied a bucket of ice water over his head.

His hands slid onto her upper arms and locked

there, holding her away from him and the delicious pleasure of her body against his.

'I am not so sure about the "lucky" bit, Dee. Right now I am in London for a few days to sort things out and run a few classes, then Paris for a month at most. Then I'm off to Canberra…and my diary is full for the next eighteen months. Constant pressure. And all the while I feel as though I am running and running and not getting anywhere.'

'Then maybe you should stand still long enough to look around and see what you have achieved,' she said. Dee tilted her head to one side. 'Somewhere along the way to being the best, I think you forgot the fun part. But I think that funny and creative side of Sean is still inside you, all ready to get excited about new things and have the best time of his life.'

Stretching up onto tiptoes, she kissed him on the lips. 'You deserve it.'

She stepped back and patted him twice on the chest. Then she laughed. 'And now it is time to head back down stairs before I embarrass myself even more.' And she moved a step backwards with a smile.

He frowned, nodded just once and muttered something under his breath along the lines of what he did for the firm. Then he lifted his head, turned towards the door and presented the crook of his arm for her to latch onto. 'Shall we go to the ball, princess? Your audience awaits.'

CHAPTER ELEVEN

Tea, glorious tea. A celebration of teas from around the world.

Astrologers have long used tea leaves to predict the future. Try it for yourself by leaving a little tea in the bottom of your tea pot with the tea leaves. Stir the brew three times, empty the tea pot into your saucer, then inspect the pattern the leaves make in the cup. Each specific pattern has a special meaning.

From *Flynn's Phantasmagoria of Tea*

Friday
A week later

SEAN STROLLED INTO the bar at the Beresford Riverside and nodded to the head barman who was serving after-dinner drinks to guests wandered in from the dining room.

The light strains of a cocktail piano could just

be heard in the background against the chatter and laughter from the guests.

He quickly scanned the bar and lounge area to see if Dee was still there. She had called him a couple of times during the afternoon to let him know that Prakash and his team had done an amazing job and all of the last minute worries that had kept her awake were sorted.

The tea festival was all set to go tomorrow.

Then he heard her laughter ring out from a table of Japanese guests who had clustered around the tables next to the long patio doors which led onto the landscaped gardens.

Ribbons of white outdoor lights trailed over the budding branches of the cherry trees which Dee had enjoyed over the past few days.

The first smile of the day slid over his mouth. Hell. His first smile all week. Last minute presentations, flying visits to France with his dad and two days scouting for locations in Scotland meant that he had hardly seen Dee since the night of the dinner.

He missed her like crazy.

Dee was sitting at the table, and spread out in front of her was what looked like a makeshift kitchen. White saucers from the kitchen were scattered all around her, and on each was a tiny sample of what looked to Sean like clippings from the evergreen plants outside in the garden but were no doubt some example of specialist tea leaves.

Whatever they were, the hotel guests seemed enthralled. They were picking up the saucers, sniffing, tasting and chatting away with enormous enthusiasm and clear delight. Nodding, delighted, bewitched.

Because at the centre of it all was Dee.

Sean paused at the bar and leant on the rail, happy just to watch the woman he had come to find.

Her long, sensitive fingers flitted above the table gesturing here and there, no doubt on some terribly important point about growing conditions and water temperature, and he could see the glint of gold in the bangles around her wrists.

She was wearing what for Dee probably passed for quite a conservative outfit of a fitted jacket in a knitted navy fabric which clung to her curves as she moved. But of course that was offset by a stunning scarf which shimmered in shades of blues and greens, highlighting her fair complexion, and even though her head was down he knew that those pale-green eyes were going to be totally enchanting.

This was the real Dee. Sharing her passion and enjoying every second of it.

The Dee he had fallen for the minute he had looked up from a tea room floor and was sucked into oblivion by those eyes. Why wouldn't he? She was stunning.

Recognition came flooding in, and instead of pushing it away Sean held it in his mind and treasured it like a precious gift that he had never expected to receive but adored.

He was falling for Dee Flynn. In a big way. This was way beyond attraction. He cared about her and wanted to be with her, in every way possible.

And the very idea shocked him and terrified him so badly that he could only stand there and take it like a sock in the jaw.

His life had been a roller coaster for so many years, he had forgotten what it felt like to make connections with people and form bonds that went beyond business transactions, contracts and meetings in windowless white rooms.

But why now?

He slid silently onto a high-boy leather bar stool.

This was the way he was going to remember her.

He had only been standing there for a few minutes in silent ogling when he saw her head lift and her back straighten.

Almost as if she knew that he was watching her. So that, when she stood up and looked over her shoulder at him, he should have been ready for the impact that seeing her smile transform into a grin that was laser-focused on him would cause.

Impossible. Nothing could have prepared him for the blast of that smile.

She had never looked lovelier. And she literally took his breath away.

Mesmerized, Sean could only watch as she excused herself with several deep bows to the guests, who returned her bows with gentle warm waves and smiles.

Oh yes, she was good.

She skipped between the tables and was at the bar in seconds.

Instantly she flung her arms around his neck as he bent down to kiss her on the cheek, much to the amusement of the hotel guests.

'You have been away far too long, Sean Beresford.'

'Agreed. Only, I think your fan club are taking our photograph on their smart phones.'

Dee peeked around Sean's back and waved back. 'Oh no, those are proper cameras. We are probably already online. But I'm not in the least ashamed. This has been a brilliant afternoon.' And, just to prove it, she went up on tiptoes and pecked him on the lips so lightly that he barely had time to register the sensation of her warm, full lips on his before she stepped back into her shoes.

'I hardly dare to ask,' he replied, but kept his arms tight around her waist. 'But could it be anything to do with the party of visiting Japanese academics?'

Dee pressed one finger to her bottom lip and tried to look innocent, but failed.

'You do know that they brought their own tea with them, don't you? The word is out Mr B— there is not one hotel in the whole of London who serves speciality Japanese green tea of the quality your guests demand and in the way they like. I think this is quite shocking news. Just imagine the impact on the hotel trade. If only you knew someone who could import some of that fine tea for you. Just imagine what a difference it could make. Now…I wonder what we can do about that?'

Then she fluttered her eyelashes at him in the most outrageous, over-the-top way and a bubble of laughter burst up from deep inside his gut and exploded into a real belly-laugh. The kind of laugh which turned heads and made the barman look at Sean over the top of his spectacles.

And why not? It had been far too long since he had laughed out loud—really laughed.

He had almost forgotten what it felt like, which was more than sad. It was a judgement of the life that he had chosen for himself and had never stopped to question—a roller coaster of work and travel, then more work and more travel, which never stopped long enough for him to get off and see the view now and then. It was too fast, and the highs and lows were so exhilarating, that it was impossible to look anywhere else but straight ahead because he never knew what was going to happen next.

It was a life that was as addictive as it was exhausting. A rush of daily adventure and excitement that called for his total focus and attention.

That was why he had been so attracted to Sasha.

They loved the hotel trade, and the rush of pulling off seemingly impossible projects and delighting his father and their hotel guests along the way. Sasha had been on her own roller coaster and at first they had been side by side, project to project. But slowly their tracks had simply drifted apart, further and further away, until they hadn't been able to see one another. Both of them had been strapped in and going for the adventure of their lives.

It was true. His life was one long roller-coaster ride. He had jumped on when he was sixteen and was still strapped in at thirty-one.

Almost half of his life.

Strange. He had never thought of it that way until now.

And he knew exactly who he had to thank for that.

The girl with the twinkling green eyes who was grinning up at him.

The girl who had swept into his life like a warm breeze on a cold day.

The girl who he was going to leave behind, and sooner than he had planned.

Sean slid one of his hands from her waist and onto the bar so that he could lean forward slightly. He inhaled the light floral fragrance that she was wearing like the aroma of a fine wine. Intoxicating and provocative. Heady and enticing. Daring him to find out if her skin tasted as delicious as the aroma promised.

'I still haven't forgiven you for texting me when you knew that Tuesday was our Bake and Bitch Club night. The girls were scandalized by that sort of suggestive language.'

'How could I forget our first anniversary? And you did call me brazen last week. I have a reputation to maintain, young lady,' he whispered into her ear in a voice that was not meant to be overheard, especially by the hotel staff.

Her eyes met his without hesitation or excuse. Beguiling. Honest. True. And, oh, so magical.

'I know. And I am certainly not complaining,' she said.

Sean swallowed down a lump in his throat.

Dee was so close. So very close. Her gaze was locked onto his face, as though it was the most fascinating thing that she had ever seen, and he almost flinched with the loss when a guest sidled up behind them at the bar.

'That colour looks great on you.' He smiled. 'Stylish and…' He paused and, when he was sure that she was looking at him, silently mouthed the word 'hot' before slipping off the bar stool and grabbing her hand.

Her eyebrows lifted and she replied with a girly giggle and a small shoulder-wiggle, which was so endearing that he had to distract himself by focusing on the way her fingers felt clasped inside his.

Time to move to something less likely to scandalize his staff.

'I think it's about time you showed me what you have been up to in my conference suite. Don't you?'

Dee paused outside the main doors to the conference room where she had spent most of the day with Prakash, and a stream of porters, delivery drivers and other people who she had never met before but who somehow seemed to be able to transform her sketches and lists into reality.

She raised one hand, palm upwards. 'Now, it might come as a bit of a shock. So prepare yourself.'

Sean nodded just once. 'I have been through

everything, from Mardi Gras to beer festivals. I can handle it.'

Dee stretched out her hand towards the brass door plate, then lifted it back and whirled around on her heel. 'First of all, I should say that Prakash and the team were amazing. Just amazing. And they did it all in one day! Totally brilliant, in fact. I couldn't have done any of this without them… And now I am babbling, because I'm so excited and it's wonderful, and did I say that it is amazing and the festival is tomorrow and…?'

'Dee.' Sean smiled and gently rested a hand on each of her shoulders. 'I spoke to Prakash. He helped, but this is your idea. Your design, your colour scheme, your concept. So I know that it is going to be wonderful.'

'Perhaps you should come back tomorrow when the exhibitors are setting up. There will be such a buzz.'

Sean looked over her shoulder into the middle distance and seemed about to say something, but changed his mind, turned back and lowered his head so that his nose was almost pressed against hers. He spoke in a jokey, firm voice.

'Dee. I want the full tour and I want it now.'

'You are so bossy!'

'I know. But that's why you like me.'

'Really? Is that the reason? I thought it was your snazzy ties and shiny shoes.'

'They only add to the allure. And you're putting off the inevitable. What is it? Why don't you want me to see your design? You know that I am going to, one way or another. '

'Yes. I know. It is your hotel. It's just that…' She sucked in a breath then exhaled on one long string of words. 'I am seriously nervous because this is the biggest thing that I have ever done on my own and I know that it's mad but my whole future depends on this being a big success.'

Then she stopped, but Sean kept looking at her with that smile on his face, as though he was waiting for her to carry on.

Then without waiting another second he stepped forward, pushed open the doors to the conference suite with both hands and stood to one side.

Then he nodded towards the space behind him, reached out and grabbed her hand. 'Come on.' He smiled. 'Show me what you have done. Show me what your imagination has created. Share it with me. Please.'

For the next ten minutes Sean walked slowly around the room as Dee explained each of the display panels in turn, starting with the history of tea production, then slowly walking from stand to stand.

She didn't need to. But he liked hearing her voice, so he let her carry on.

The whole room was decorated in co-ordinating shades of green with stencils of green tea leaves against cream, pale gold and emerald green. There were plenty of stands for the exhibitors, power points, fresh water dispensers. And a portable professional kitchen. All ready for the morning. He couldn't have been prouder.

'So this is where the magic is going to happen. I love it. Professional, elegant and attractive. It's a hit!'

'Do you really think so?' Dee screwed up her mouth.

'It looks fresh and inviting. And the colour scheme is great.'

His hands moved in gentle circles on her shoulders, up and down her arms, and slowly, slowly, the stiffness in Dee's neck relaxed and she felt her shoulders drop down from around her ears.

'You must think that I am a total idiot,' she chuckled. 'All of this work for a one-day festival of tea. The world will not end if nobody turns up to drink the tea and buy the china. And on Sunday I can go back to the tea rooms and carry on as normal. I know that; I've known that from the start. But being with you and working in the hotel here has given me so many ideas for new projects, and new ways I can sell my blended tea, I can hardly sleep at night. It is so exciting. So, whatever happens tomorrow, thank you, Sean. Thank you for helping me.'

His response was to step forward and gather her into his arms, holding her tight against his pristine shirt, not caring that he was crushing his superb suit jacket in the process. Holding her with such tenderness and warmth that she melted against him with a gentle sigh. Instantly his chin slid down and rested on the top of her hair, and his arms relaxed their grip and rested gently on her back.

It had been so long since she had felt so close to another human being. Lottie and the girls were her best friends, and she loved every one of them, but this was different, felt different; this was special.

It had been ages since her last boyfriend in the tea house. Years of watching other girls go on the dating scene, and comforting them with tea and cake as each broken heart had healed and they'd gone out again so full of hope.

Not for her. She did not want that emotional destruction. She knew that she was too different for most men. Too quirky. Too obsessed. Too unusual.

She was not the girl that the boys in catering school introduced to their parents. She was the girl they dated until someone better came along. And it had taken her a while to realize that she was not putting up with being second best. And she never would.

Until Sean had shown her that she was a woman a man could admire and want to be with.

Sean had chosen her. Picked her out. Made her feel special. Made her feel that she was capable of running her own business and making her dream come true.

Sean. The man who was holding her in his arms at that moment.

The man who meant the world to her. But she was too afraid to tell him.

She revelled in every sensation, her eyes closed,

locking each tiny moment into her memory. The heady aroma of Sean's body wash or aftershave blended with the subtle scent of laundry lavender, and a lot of Sean that only a long day in a hot office could produce. If only she could bottle that aroma, she would never be lonely again.

This was one man who had listened to what she wanted and helped her make it happen in a way which was even better than she had imagined.

She wanted this moment to last as long as possible. She wanted to remember what these little bubbles of happiness felt like.

'You are most welcome,' he replied, the sound muffled as he spoke into her hair, but the sound reverberated through her skull and came to rest in the centre of her heart. Where they exploded into a firework display of light and colour.

Exploded with such force that they made her shuffle back a little so that she could look up into Sean's face and trace the line of his jaw with her fingers. Her reward was to see his eyes flutter just a little as her fingers slid down onto his neck and throat.

This man had pressed buttons that she did not even know that she had.

'If you ever see that Frank Evans, be sure to thank him for me.' She grinned. 'Because it seems to me that I came out with a pretty good deal.'

Sean rested his hands on her hips and nodded. 'True. The Beresford Riverside is a rather more impressive venue than the Beresford Richmond Square, and you did get it for the same price. That was what you were referring to…wasn't it?'

Dee dropped her head forward onto his chest with a short laugh, only too aware that she was blushing and her neck was probably a lovely shade of scarlet.

When she did dare to lift her head, Sean was looking at her, his eyes more blue than grey in the artificial lighting above their heads, and as her eyes locked onto his the intensity of that gaze seemed to penetrate her skin.

For one fraction of a second all the need and passion of this remarkable man was revealed for her to see.

In one single look.

It took her breath away and she lifted her head higher. So high that, when his head tilted and he pressed his lips against her forehead, and then her temple, she was ready.

More than ready.

She was waiting for his kiss.

She had been waiting all day for his kiss, to see him again and to hear his voice.

And it had been totally, totally, worth the wait.

Sean took one step forward, and before Dee realized what was happening he wrapped his hand around the back of her neck, his fingers working into her hair as he pressed his mouth against hers, pushing open her full lips, moving back and forth, his breath fast and heavy on her face.

His mouth was tender, gentle but firm, as though he was holding back the floodgates of a passion which was on the verge of breaking through and overwhelming them both.

She felt that potential, she trembled at the thought of it, and at that moment she knew that she wanted it as much as he did.

Her eyes closed as she wrapped her arms around his back and leaned into the kiss, kissing him back, revelling in the sensual heat of Sean's body as it pressed against hers. Closer, closer, until his arms were taking the weight of her body, enclosing her in his loving, sweet embrace. The pure physicality of the man was almost overpowering.

The scent of his muscular body pressed ever so gently against her combined with the heavenly scent that she knew now was unique to him.

It filled her senses with an intensity that she had never felt in the embrace of any other man in her life. He was totally overwhelming. Intoxicating. And totally, totally delicious.

And, just when Dee thought that there could be nothing more pleasurable in this world, his kiss deepened. It was as though he wanted to take everything that she was able to give him, and without a second of doubt she surrendered to the hot spice of the taste of his mouth and tongue.

This was the kind of kiss she had never known. The connection between them was part of it, but this went beyond friendship and common interests. This was a kiss to signal the start of something new. The kind of kiss where each of them was opening up their most intimate secrets and deepest feelings for the other person to see.

The heat, the intensity, the desire of this man, was all there, exposed for her to see ,when she eventually opened her eyes and broke the connection. Shuddering. Trembling. Grateful that he was holding her up on her wobbly legs.

Then he pulled away, the faint stubble on his chin grazing across her mouth as he lifted his face to kiss her eyes, brow and temple.

It took a second for her to catch her breath before she felt able to open her eyes, only to find Sean was still looking at her, his forehead still pressed against hers. A smile warmed his face as he moved his hand down to stroke her cheek.

He knew. He knew the effect that his kiss was having on her body. He had to. Her face burned with the heat coming from the point of contact between them. His heart was racing, just as hers was.

Dee slowly, slowly slid out of his embrace and almost slithered onto the floor. And by the time she was on her unsteady legs she was already missing the warmth of those arms and the heat of the fire on her face.

She had to do something to fight the intensity of the magnetic attraction that she felt for Sean at that moment. Logic screamed at her from the back of her mind: they were both single, unattached and they wanted one another.

She had never had a one-night stand in her life.

And, if she was going to do it, this was as good a place as any, except of course it would never be casual sex. Not for her. And, she suspected, not for Sean either.

Would it be so ridiculous if they spent the night together?

Sean gently drew her back towards him so that their faces were only inches apart at the same height.

His hand moved to her cheek, pushing her hair back over her left ear, his thumb on her jaw as his eyes scanned her face, back and forth.

Her eyes opened wide and she drunk him in— all of him. The way his hair curled dark and heavy around his ears and neck; the suntanned crease lines on the sides of his mouth and eyes. And those eyes—those amazing blue eyes which burned bright as they smiled at her.

She could look at that face all day and not get tired of it. In fact, it was turning out to be her favourite occupation.

Sean was temptation personified. And all she had to do was reach out and taste just how delicious that temptation truly was.

Did he know what effect he was having on her? How much he was driving her wild?

Probably.

Panting for breath, she rested her head on his chest, listening to the sound of Sean's heart under the fine cloth, feeling the hot flood of blood in his veins and the pressure of his fists against her back. She could have stayed there all night but suddenly the silence of their private space was broken by the loud ringtone from the mobile phone inside Sean's jacket pocket.

'That can wait,' he whispered and carried on stroking her hair. 'Now, tell me about the tea. What delicious aromas can the hotel expect...?' But he never got to continue because his phone rang again, and this time is was a different ringtone.

'Oh, I don't believe it.' He sighed, stood back, tugged out the phone and checked the caller ID. 'It's my dad's personal line.' He shook his head. 'I am so sorry about this. Stay right where you are. Two minutes.'

Dee sat down at the reception table just inside the door and watched Sean stride out into the main hotel space, the phone pressed to his ear. He was pacing up and down, one hand pressed against the back of his neck in a nervous gesture that she had seen him use a couple of times.

She pressed her fingers to her mouth, which was feeling slightly numb, and covered a chuckle. He didn't even realize that he was doing it.

Dee stood up and strolled into the kitchens between the display areas. She was just about to pour some water when one of the flyers dropped to the floor in the cool breeze from one of the floor-to-ceiling sliding glass doors that was still half-open.

But, instead of closing it, Dee stepped onto the stone courtyard area outside the conference room and slowly inhaled the cool evening air.

After the heat of the past hour it felt deliciously cool on her hot skin.

In the cool February air she could see the lights of the high-tech businesses, city offices and homes which lined the opposite bank of the river Thames. The hotel was partly shaded from the riverside public footpath by landscaped grounds and trees creating a calm and open feel.

It was exactly what she wanted: no white plastic

underground basements, just a well-lit and modern space which opened up to the air whenever she wanted.

There was a faint rustling from the room behind her, and Dee looked over one shoulder as Sean came to join her on the terrace. His face was in shadow but she would recognize his shape anywhere.

A soft and silky Sean-warmed suit jacket was draped over her shoulders and she snuggled into it as a cold shiver ran down her spine.

She could feel the warmth of his chest through the many layers of clothing as he pressed his body against her back and wrapped his arms around her waist so that they were both facing the river and the superb view of the city spread out in front of them.

It was as if they were the only people alive at that moment and in that space.

Instinctively she leant backwards so that the back of her head was resting on his chest. The beat of his heart was steady in her ears, then faster.

She did not need to hear it to know that it grew faster for her.

Sean was breathing faster, his pace matching her own.

'No stars tonight,' she whispered and pointed up at the clouds which had already covered the crescent moon. 'But you can still make a wish if you like. You don't need a shooting star to have your dream come true. I know that now. So tonight is your turn.'

His reply was a hoarse whisper and she felt his hands slip away from around her waist as he spoke. 'I wish I could. But I can't. In fact, I have to go and get packed straight away.'

Dee slowly turned around in the circle of his arms so that they were facing one another, and suddenly a shiver ran across her shoulders. In the light from the room she could see the new harsh lines on Sean's face. All easy chatter and smiles had been wiped away as if they had never been there.

'Packed? I don't understand. You are not due in Paris for another few days and you've only just got back. You told me that yourself. You don't need to get packed tonight.'

He licked his lips and looked at her, his gaze darting across her face. 'I thought that I had at least a week. But that telephone call changed everything.'

Sean lifted his chin as though he was preparing himself.

'I am sorry, Dee, but I am booked on a flight to Chicago. We have an emergency at the new Beresford hotel we opened at Christmas and they need me to help sort things out. I have to go. And I have to go tonight. So you see, I'll be gone by the morning.'

Dee stepped backwards and out of his arms, her fingers running down his shirt sleeves so that she was clinging on to him with only a thin layer of fine cotton.

'Tonight? Do you really have to? We have worked so hard on this together. I…I was hoping that you would be here for the festival tomorrow.'

Dee turned and stared out into the dark night. Her eyes fixed on the movement of the wind in the trees that she could just see in the light from the hotel. There was a cold, damp wind blowing up from the river and she could feel the moisture cooling her face. But it didn't help to cool the fire burning inside her head.

She felt as though she had been caught in some

kind of tornado that had been spinning her round and round from the moment she'd met Sean. Spinning so fast that she had never truly had the chance to get her feet back on the ground.

She had always known that his work in London was temporary, but Paris was only a few hours away by train. They might have had a chance to stay in touch and to stay close. If they worked at it.

If they both wanted it enough.

If he wanted it as much as she did.

He was leaving.

Just as her parents had decided to leave behind the cold, grey British winters and go back to the sunshine and the life that they loved. Just as her friends from catering college had left for jobs all over the world. Just as Josh had gone back to his real girlfriend and left his stand-in, second-best girl standing on the pavement outside his apartment reeling from what the hell had just happened.

She had coped with saying goodbye and managing the shock. And she still had Lottie and Gloria and the girls in the baking club. She could cope with saying goodbye to Sean. She was going to have to; he wasn't giving her any other choice.

It wasn't meant to be this hard.

She just wanted him to stay with her so badly.

Sean snuggled up next to her in the silence, the whole left side of his body pressed against her right side. Thigh to thigh, hip to hip and arm to arm.

She wanted to rest her head on his shoulder, and her whole body yearned to lean sideways against him for support, but she fought off the temptation.

She had to.

It was almost too much to bear when his fingers meshed with hers, locking them together in the dark.

Slowly, slowly, she found the strength to look up into the most amazing blue-grey eyes. In the bar they had been like clear, blue, fresh tropical seas, alluring, tempting and begging her to dive in. But now they were dark and stormy. Dangerous.

The warmth had been replaced with an intensity and concern that she had never seen before.

It was all there in the hard lines of his handsome face. The face that she had come to love so much over the past week or so, though she did not dare admit that to herself.

The planes of his face were brought into sharp contrast by the light from the room.

She had been so wrong to imagine that the son of Tom Beresford would have an easy office job handed down by his father.

Sean worked so very hard. And she admired him for that. But why now? Why did he have to go tonight?

'What kind of emergency is it?' she asked in a voice which was quaking a lot more than she wanted. 'Not another flood, I hope.'

His lips parted and he took in a long, shuddering breath before replying in a low, hoarse voice which to her ears seemed heavy with regret and concern.

'No; worse. Food poisoning. Rob thinks that it's a norovirus, and he is already on site working with the authorities, but the hotel is closed and guests are on lockdown. And I really do not want to talk about kitchen detox at this precise moment.'

His fingers clenched around hers and Dee tried focusing on the flickering lights on the riverbank but she could sense every tiny movement of his body which made vision a little difficult.

Her eyes fluttered closed as he took a tighter hold of her fingers and stepped away and she instantly yearned to have his body next to her again.

Instead he gently lifted her hand to his mouth and kissed the back of her knuckles, forcing her to look up into his face.

'I wanted to be there tomorrow. To share your triumph. Because that is what it is going to be—a triumph.'

His head tilted slightly and one side of his mouth lifted up into a half-smile. 'You are going to be amazing. I know it. And Prakash has promised me a full report with video and photos.'

'Video?' She spluttered. 'That wasn't on the list.'

His gaze was focused on her hair and he casually lifted a stray strand of her lop-sided fringe and popped it behind her ear in a gesture so tender and caring that she almost cried at the pleasure of it.

'I ticked all of the optional extras on the checklist for you. Courtesy of the hotel management.'

'Wow,' she whispered and was rewarded with a quick nod of reply and a flash of a smile.

'Sean?' she asked in a quiet voice, and she closed the tiny gap between them. 'How long are you going to be away in Chicago? A week? Two? Then you are going to be in Paris, right?'

'I don't know. Weeks, most likely. As for Paris?

There is no way I can handle that now. My dad is going to take over the project and find another manager.'

Dee exhaled a long sigh of relief. 'That's great. So when are you coming back to London? I will have so much to tell you.'

His head dropped down so that his forehead was almost touching hers and she could feel the heat of his breath on her face.

So that there was nowhere for her to escape to when he formed the words that she had been dreading.

'You don't understand, Dee. Paris is cancelled. My next assignment is in Brazil for a couple of months and then back to Australia in the autumn. I'm not coming back to London.'

CHAPTER TWELVE

Tea, glorious tea. A celebration of teas from around the world.
A simple infusion of chamomile flowers can help to relax the nerves and aid in sleep by creating a general feeling of relaxation.

From *Flynn's Phantasmagoria of Tea*

'NOT COMING BACK? Then I only want to know the answer to one question—and I don't want to hear it over the phone or in an email. Don't treat me like one of your managers. Talk to me. I want to hear your answer here and now. In person. To my face.'

She pressed both hands flat against his shirt so that the racing beat of his heart flittered up through her fingertips.

He was hurting just as much as she was.

'Do you want to see me again, Sean? Because if you don't it would be better if you told me now and be done with it, so that…' She lifted her chin. 'So that we can both get on with our lives.'

'Do I want to be with you? Oh, Dee.'

His right hand came up and flicked his suit jacket onto a patio table, exposing her skin to the cold night air, and instantly she could feel her nipples pebble with alertness. His long fingers slid down the whole length of her body from her neck, down the treacherous front of her jacket to her hips and back again.

Without asking for permission or forgiveness he slipped his warm hand up inside her jacket and cupped her breast. His thumb moved over her nipple with the perfect amount of pressure to fire up every nerve in her body.

But Sean had found the perfect distraction, kissing her forehead, temple and throat with such exquisitely gentle kisses that any idea of a question was driven out her mind as her desire for him built with each touch of his lips on hers.

And, just when she thought that her legs were going to buckle, his fingers slid away until her entire breast was being cupped by his hand and her bra was redundant and getting in the way of the exquisite pleasure.

Then slowly, slowly, his hand slid lower onto the bare skin at her waist and rested there for a second before moving away.

Arms wrapped around his head, Dee hung onto Sean as he wrapped both arms around her and held her to him.

She could feel the supressed power of his answer pressing against her hip and his short, fast breaths on her neck, fighting, fighting for control.

'Oh, Sean,' she whispered through a closed throat, and she dropped her head down to the safety and warmth of his broad chest.

They must have stayed there for several minutes, but time seemed to stand still, and it was Sean who broke the silence.

'I have been down this road before, Dee. My last girlfriend was so patient and we tried so hard to make it work. But in the end we were both worn down with the constant struggle to make time for one another between going back and forwards to the airport. It was exhausting. And it killed a great friendship. I don't want that to happen to us, Dee. Not to us.'

He was stroking her hair now, running his fingers back from her forehead. 'It could be six months before I get back here, and even then it would only be for a flying visit. There will always be some crisis somewhere, like tonight, which needs me to fly out at a moment's notice. I can't plan holidays or down time. You deserve better than that. A lot better.'

Dee looked up into his face and blinked, her mouth part open. 'No. I deserve you. All of you.'

Her words stung like ice on hot skin, burning into his brain and leaving a scar.

'The last thing I want to do is hurt you, Dee. That's why it's better that we part now and re-member the good times.'

She laid her cheek on his shirt and dared to fi-nally find the words. 'Does it have to be that way, Sean? Is there truly nobody else in the company that can cover your job? What happens when you are ill or burnt out? You can't keep going like this for ever. You have to take a break some time.'

'Don't feel sorry for me, Dee,' he replied, his hand cupping the back of her head. 'My family are very close, we always have been, and I owe my father everything. This hotel chain is my life and I want to make it special.'

'It seems to me that you have paid your family dues, Sean. Paid in full.'

'What do you mean?

Dee forced herself to raise her head and slip backwards so that she could look up into his face. 'This is your decision to leave tonight. Not your father's. Or your brother's. Yours. You have recruited an amazing team of talented professionals who would be only too happy to take on some of those troubleshooting challenges if you gave them the chance. You have made these hotels your life—and I understand that. Look at me—the tea grower's daughter who wants to set up her own tea company. We are both following in the family trade. But maybe it's time to think hard about what you want to do with your life. And who you want to spend it with.'

Then she stood back and slowly slid her fingers from his, one finger at a time, breaking their connection with each movement as she spoke.

She stood on tiptoe, pressed her lips against his in one last, lingering kiss, then ran her finger along his jaw and smiled.

'Good luck, Sean. Goodbye and thank you for everything.'

Then she turned and walked away, back into the conference room and out of his life. Without looking back.

And this time he didn't follow her.

CHAPTER THIRTEEN

Tea, glorious tea. A celebration of teas from around the world.
The traditional treatment for shock in Britain is a steaming beaker of piping hot Indian tea with milk and plenty of sugar. This remedy should be repeated until the symptoms subside.

From *Flynn's Phantasmagoria of Tea*

Saturday

HER BEST FRIEND slid a plate in front of her in the early-morning light streaming in through her bedroom window.

Dee squinted over the top of her extra-strong English Breakfast at the slice of a tall extravaganza of green-and vanilla-coloured sponge layers.

It was very green. And smelt of a florist shop. And no amount of strong tea was going to be able to wash down that amount of sugar and fat.

'I am calling this my tea festival special. It's a

Lady Grey flavoured opera cake with a rosewater cream filling. What do you think?'

'Think? I am too tired to think, and my taste buds are fried. Thanks, Lottie. I am sure it will be a brilliant hit. It looks wonderful, but I just can't face it at the moment. Way too nervous.'

Lottie rubbed the back of Dee's shoulder and kissed the top of her head.

'I had a feeling that it might be a bit over the top for six a.m. Did you get any sleep at all?'

Dee shook her head. 'Maybe a couple of hours at most. Kept waking up and couldn't get back to sleep again.'

'Never fear. I have donuts, and cheese and ham croissants. The breakfast of champions. I'll be right back.'

'You're my hero,' Dee replied and smiled after Lottie as she took the stairs down to the bakery from her apartment.

Her hero.

Dee stretched out her arms on the small table, dropped her head onto her hands and closed her eyes.

She was exhausted and her day had not started yet.

This was the most important event of her career. Months of planning. Weeks of phone calls, emails, checklists and constant to-ing and fro-ing from the hotel. And it all came down to this.

One girl sitting alone in her bedroom, drinking tea in her dressing gown. Feeling as though she had just gone through twelve rounds of a professional boxing match and lost.

Every part of her body ached, her head was thumping and she could easily fall asleep sitting upright in this hard chair.

Little wonder.

Lottie thought that she had stayed awake because of nerves about what today would bring. And that was true. But it was not the real reason she had tossed and turned until her duvet was on the floor and her sheet a tangled mess, wrapped around her like a restricting cocoon.

Sean. All she could think about, every time she closed her eyes, was Sean.

How he looked, tasted, smelt and felt. Sean.

And the worst thing?

The more she thought about what he had said to her, and repeated their conversation over and over in her head, the more she knew in her heart that he had been right to walk away and end what they had.

Sean had let her go rather than prolong the agony of always expecting her to take a place in the long line of other priorities that came with his position in the company.

He had done a noble thing.

He had given her up so that she could find someone who was able to put her first.

She *did* deserve better than to feel that she was always going to take second place in his list of priorities.

She *was* worthy of having someone to be there when she needed them. Like today.

Her parents had always put work first before her. Not because they intended to hurt her; far from it. They loved what they did and had explained many times that they wanted to be happy so that she could share that happiness.

Shame that it had never made it any easier to accept.

Shame that she would have loved to have Sean with her today of all days. To share her excitement and sense of achievement. To share her joy with the man she had come to love. The man she still wanted to be with.

The first man that she wanted to be with.

This was all so new and bewildering. Oh, there had been plenty of teenage crushes before. And broken hearts galore. But the way she felt this morning was something very different.

It was if she had tasted something so wonderful that it was terrifying to think that she might never taste it again.

Dee raised her body back to a sitting position and peered glassy-eyed at the photograph of her smiling parents, and Lottie's bizarre but no doubt totally delicious cake, and a small chuckle made her shoulders rise and fall.

Even in the daily mayhem that constituted her mad world, falling for one of heirs to the Beresford hotel dynasty was surely the craziest.

She picked up the fork, speared a small chunk of cake and closed her lips around it, savouring the different flavours. Letting her tongue and the sensitive taste buds that made her job possible do the work before chewing for a moment and swallowing it down.

'Oh, you tried the cake. Brave woman. Go on. Hit me with it.'

Lottie marched into her bedroom with a tray, sat down on the bed and bared her teeth in fear of the honest review.

Dee raised her eyebrows and licked her lips. 'You put ground black pepper in the cream to off-set the rosewater. And I am tasting orange zest and a hint of cloves and cardamom in the tea-scented sponge.'

'Absolutely. I knew that you would get it. So? Lady Grey or a green tea?'

Dee took the tray out of Lottie's hands. 'Green. But a special one. This is good. This is very good. Congratulations, Miss Rosemount. You have just succeeded in creating one of the toughest tea-matching challenges I have ever come across. Please accept this hand-crafted medal.'

'This is not a medal. It's an exhibitors badge for the tea festival.'

'Well, you don't think I would face the raven-ous cake-eating hordes without you there to serve it and bask in the glory, did you? And, after all, we can't have tea without the cake to go with it! Foolish girl.'

Then Dee's smile faded and she reached out and took Lottie's hand. 'Can you come with me? Just for a couple of hours. Please? Gloria and the gang will look after the tea rooms. I just… I just need a pal by my side today. It turns out that being a tea magnate is not half as much fun when you don't have someone to share the excitement with. And I didn't expect that. I didn't expect that at all.'

Sean dug into his pocket, pulled out his mobile phone and dialled the number with shaking fingers.

He had been up most of the night, talking to Rob, who was fighting health inspectors in Chicago, and his father, who was fighting to stay awake after two hours of pacing back and forth going over the business plans for the hotel chain and where Sean was going in his career. And his life.

Please still be there.

Please answer.

Please don't throw the phone out of the window when you see who is calling you. Please take this call.

The only voice in the world he wanted to hear whispered, 'Hello?'

'Dee. It's Sean. I'm standing outside the tea rooms but I won't come in unless you want me to. Please say yes.'

The fraction of a second before she replied seemed like an eternity. 'Sean? What do you mean you are outside the tea rooms? I thought that you would be in Chicago by now.'

'Long story, but I'd like to tell you about it in person instead of on the pavement in the dark at the crack of dawn.'

'Okay. Yes, Lottie will let you in.'

It took Sean three seconds to give a very startled Lottie a quick wave, then bound up the stairs two at a time and stand puffing and panting outside Dee's bedroom.

His hand stretched out towards the door handle. And then he snatched it back.

Eyes closed, he blew out a long, deep breath, his head suddenly dizzy with doubt as the blood surged in his veins.

What was he doing here? What if she said, thanks, but no thanks? This was crazy.

He loved this woman and he had been willing

to let her go because he was afraid of changing his life? Mad.

For once he was going to risk their future happiness on a crazy decision to trust his heart instead of his head.

And what if she said yes? She could be committing herself to a life where he could be on the road or in a different hotel most of the year. Was that fair?

Yes. Because he was just as determined to show Dee that he was able to give her a fraction of the love she felt for him.

And he had to do it now. Or never. Perhaps that was why he felt so naked. Exposed.

Sean straightened his back and just prepared to knock, but at the very second he did so there was movement on the other side of the door, and the handle turned on its own and cracked open an inch, then wider…and Dee was standing there.

Her eyes locked onto his as she looked at him with the kind of intensity that seemed to knock the oxygen from his lungs.

Then those eyes smiled and he took in the full effect of that beautiful face. No camera in the world could have captured the look on Dee's face at this moment.

He felt as though the air would explode with the electricity in the air between them.

'Hi,' she whispered. 'Has something happened to bring you back? Are you okay?' There was so much love and concern in her voice that any doubts Sean had about what he had to do next were wiped away.

Sean stretched out his hand and stroked her cheek, his eyes never leaving hers.

'I haven't stopped thinking about what you said. And you were right. Leaving last night was my decision. So I did something about it.'

Sean breathed in, his heart thudding so loudly that he suspected that she must be hearing it from where she was standing so quietly, dressed in her kimono. 'I know now that I will always love you, Dervla Flynn, and it doesn't matter where I am in the world.' He licked her lips. 'I want to be with you. Love you.'

Her mouth opened to reply but he pressed one finger on her lips and smiled, breaking the terror. 'You see, I'm not as brave as you are. As soon as I left you last night, I knew that I couldn't leave the woman I have fallen in love with without try-ing to come up with some options.'

He grinned at her and slid forward so that both of his hands were cupped around her face as tears pricked her eyes. 'I love you way too much to let you go. I need you, Dee. I need you so much. Nothing else comes close. What would you say if I told you that I would be working out of London for the next twelve months?'

Her reply was to fall into his arms and he swept her up, holding her body tight, tight, before tilt-ing his open mouth onto hers in a hot, hot kiss.

He cupped her face with both of his hands, his thumbs wiping away tears and water from her cheeks, and then he poured into his kiss the pas-sion and devotion, the fear and doubts, which came with giving your heart to another human being.

'I didn't expect to be saying this standing in a cake shop, but it doesn't change a thing. I am so in love with you.'

'Oh, Sean. I wasn't sure I could go through with today without you. Can you forgive me? I have been such an idiot. Of course your family need you. You love them and want to do the right thing. I know what that's like.'

'Better than you think. I have done something rash—there's a limo on the way to the airport at this very minute to collect two very special first-class passengers from a flight from Sri Lanka. I knew that you wanted your parents with you today to see all that you have done. Are you okay with that?'

'Seriously?' she asked, stunned. 'You flew my parents to London for the festival? You did that for me?'

He nodded. 'Seriously.' His thumb was still moving across her cheek. 'It's time that I met your parents. Because I am thinking of taking a break for a couple of months and Sri Lanka is on my list of destinations. If you come with me.'

'Oh, Sean. Do you mean it? Yes? Oh, I love you so much.'

He closed his eyes and pressed his forehead to hers, his entire world contained within his arms.

They were still standing there, kissing passion-ately, when there was the sound of loud voices breaking into their private world. Lottie had opened up downstairs and the first customers had arrived.

'But what about your work? Chicago? Brazil?'

'I had a long conference call with my dad and Rob last night, and we have agreed to give some senior managers a chance to show us what they can do. Plus, my dad offered me a new job this week. Could be challenging.'

'Difficult?'

'Very.' He grinned. 'Apparently he needs a new manager for the Richmond Square hotel who can fit in a bit of training now and then. Within walking distance of this cake shop and the woman I've fallen in love with. And all the tea I can drink. How could I say no?'

* * * * *

Mills & Boon® Large Print
June 2014

A BARGAIN WITH THE ENEMY
Carole Mortimer

A SECRET UNTIL NOW
Kim Lawrence

SHAMED IN THE SANDS
Sharon Kendrick

SEDUCTION NEVER LIES
Sara Craven

WHEN FALCONE'S WORLD STOPS TURNING
Abby Green

SECURING THE GREEK'S LEGACY
Julia James

AN EXQUISITE CHALLENGE
Jennifer Hayward

TROUBLE ON HER DOORSTEP
Nina Harrington

HEIRESS ON THE RUN
Sophie Pembroke

THE SUMMER THEY NEVER FORGOT
Kandy Shepherd

DARING TO TRUST THE BOSS
Susan Meier

0514 Rom LP

Mills & Boon® Large Print
July 2014

A PRIZE BEYOND JEWELS
Carole Mortimer

A QUEEN FOR THE TAKING?
Kate Hewitt

PRETENDER TO THE THRONE
Maisey Yates

AN EXCEPTION TO HIS RULE
Lindsay Armstrong

THE SHEIKH'S LAST SEDUCTION
Jennie Lucas

ENTHRALLED BY MORETTI
Cathy Williams

THE WOMAN SENT TO TAME HIM
Victoria Parker

THE PLUS-ONE AGREEMENT
Charlotte Phillips

AWAKENED BY HIS TOUCH
Nikki Logan

ROAD TRIP WITH THE ELIGIBLE BACHELOR
Michelle Douglas

SAFE IN THE TYCOON'S ARMS
Jennifer Faye

0614 Rom LP

Discover more romance at

www.millsandboon.co.uk

- 💜 WIN great prizes in our exclusive competitions

- 💜 BUY new titles before they hit the shops

- 💜 BROWSE new books and REVIEW your favourites

- 💜 SAVE on new books with the Mills & Boon® Bookclub™

- 💜 DISCOVER new authors

PLUS, to chat about your favourite reads, get the latest news and find special offers:

- Find us on facebook.com/millsandboon
- Follow us on twitter.com/millsandboonuk
- 💜 Sign up to our newsletter at millsandboon.co.uk